For my daughters and my parents, who encouraged and helped me tirelessly. And for my 'Sissy' who was the best coach ever.

For Mother Powell, without whom I would have never arrived at this point.

Chapter 1

    Chloe waited, well out of sight beyond the sill of the window. Waited silently, watching. Finally the girl appeared, her shadow preceding her in the late afternoon sunlight, slowly travelling down the dusty street out into the greenness of the field at the end of the side lane. She was unaware that her watcher had now become her follower. Footsteps lightly pacing the small prints in the dusty soil, the girl walked quickly to the far edge of the field to the line of boulders which divided the field from the sky. She perched on the largest of them, drew her pad from her satchel and gave a deep sigh of satisfaction as she began to sketch the magic of the deepening afternoon as dusk overwhelmed the small town and dry fields, turning everything into art as streaks of pink and orange raced each other across the sky. Chloe watched the girl quietly, hunkered down, cushioned on her bulky skirts. She was a small figure in the shadow of the one large tree on the edge of the field. There was no need for concealment. The girl was so taken by her sketches; she never noticed the small young girl watching her. Finally as the deepening dusk turned the sky to violet and the air began to cool in earnest, Chloe rose from her resting place and started trudging back to town. It would not do to get back so soon before father returned. Too many questions already.

    Nightly, Chloe wrote in her journal. She wrote about the daily wanderings of the girl with the pastels, and when the girl had escaped from the dusty flatness and small minded town to pursue her artistic dreams, Chloe wrote about other characters in the provincial farm town. Although the town appeared to be most conventional, especially to those outsiders who stepped off the train on rare occasions, it too had its element of individuality, like all small towns do. Chloe also wrote about her own growing desire to leave behind the convention and the shallowness of the town as well as the overly concerned neighbors who looked after the motherless girl and shook their heads at her apparent loneliness and friendlessness. This, of course, was far from the truth. Chloe, in her daily wanderings when her father was at work, had met some of the more unique individuals that the town preferred to ignore, and found them to be more interesting, more human and far more sympathetic than any of the good ladies who tried to make a husband out of her father.

    The years passed slowly. Chloe grew up in the absently caring confines of her home, at the edge of the dry and dusty little town called Stuflen which bordered the great expanse of gold fields that went on as far as the eye could see. Chloe's father was a banker in the square gray building which occupied the central spot in front of the town square. He kept the family in moderate prosperity. The house was weathered yet sturdy, with a broad front porch where Chloe could sit deep in the shadows of the roof overhang and think, or write. Her mother had died when Chloe was only six, leaving a period of bleakness which wrapped around the household like a winter cloak. Chloe didn't have many memories of her mother as she grew; a soft voice and warm arms were the strongest impressions. Eventually, Chloe and her three siblings adjusted to the loss, and, with the help of several consecutive house keepers, Chloe became adept at keeping the house to her father's liking. Every evening Father would walk home from the bank, on the wide busy main street, to their house on Frontage Street. Chloe was expected to make sure the household flowed in an uninterrupted and calm manner, much like it had in the years before his wife's death. Her father, a stolid and unimaginative man, was content in the knowledge that his children were happy with the roles he had planned for them. His two sons, older than Chloe, would join him at the bank, and Chloe would continue to keep house until the event of her marriage after which time her sister Mary would take up the reigns of housekeeping. He declined to believe that any one of them would need or want something more; least of all dream of leaving the town that he had made their home in so many years before.

Chloe's brothers were energetic and rambunctious boys who looked to their father admiringly and emulated him in all respects. They grew to be conscientious young men and cared deeply for their sisters. They were perfect models of their father, and were soon courted all around town by hopeful families. Shy young girls would smile as they walked down the streets. Chloe's sister, on the other hand, was far too imaginative and independent to be called conventional. Unlike Chloe in looks, she was tall and dark, where Chloe was smaller with the light honey colors of her mother. Mary's impish smile and quick temper got her into many scrapes in the school yard, which invariably were solved by the intercession of her older brothers. Chloe and Mary were close growing up, each turning to the other as the rest of the household failed to understand their feelings and thoughts. Mary shared her sister's feelings of distaste for their father's conventional life. However, as young as she was; she had yet to make her own decisions. That time would come for her as it was coming for Chloe.

After school every day while Chloe was young, she would race home to await her artist, the girl with the pastels. When the girl passed outside of the boundaries of the little town, she who captured the magic of the sunset in a few strokes of bold color, Chloe found other characters to observe, and later befriend. Chloe's dream was to escape like the girl with the pastels. She longed to dispute those good and upright citizens who whispered with scorn the girl's name after church services and meetings of the Women's Auxiliary Club. The girl's parents filled with pride when the girl became an independent and well regarded woman in the East, in such civilized places like New York where creativity was appreciated. They ignored the narrow minds which always grew apprehensive in the presence of such bearers of creativity, something Chloe was learning to do as well. Chloe knew she wasn't of this town either, and she knew that people whispered after her, and looked after her sympathetically as they tried to mold her into a conventional and practical young woman. She bore this indignity silently. Only her journals, growing thicker by the years would tell of her silent vigils by her window, observations of human nature.

As Chloe started to realize that her imagination had outgrown the boundaries of the town itself, and stretched beyond the golden waves of wheat, she spent more time wandering farther beyond the streets that she was so familiar with, which bounded her house on the edge of town and the bank, a few streets over. After fulfilling her father's desire for a neat and orderly house each morning, she would wander to the other side of the small town, not more than a twenty-five minute walk. Being sixteen, she was out of school and had little to do aside from the housekeeping. She would walk down Frontage Street, to the corner of Main every day, glance in the direction of the bank and the school, where her sister, now twelve, was sitting. After this she took a different street every day, walking slowly, watching. That was her favorite thing to do. People watching. In these rambles, she found other unique individuals who seemed to lead free and interesting lives. Women who did as they chose; and not as their father decided. Her friend Emily lived alone despite her youth at twenty-three and ran a shop. Despite her parents begging she remained steadfast in her determination to be independent and forged ahead, living in a small apartment over the shop. Then there was the old man who collected glass of every kind, from tiny pieces to broken shards of windows or jars, and made beautiful artwork from them, deaf to the cat calls and hooting from the small boys who daily came to torment him. Chloe never did find out his name, being too diffident to approach him directly. It was these people who made her determination to live her own life grow even stronger.

Chloe's other distraction was centered on the small dingy train station. The train would stop there daily, as it needed to refill its precious water for the rest of the journey eastward, as far as Chloe could see. She had always found it ironic that small and dusty Stuflen had a water tower. As she matured, she realized that perhaps it was not a lack of water which made the town seem dry but a lack of individuality. She was, in essence, identifying the town with her own feelings. She found that on rare occasions she had the pleasure of conversing with one or two of the strangers who stepped from the train. This too filled some time in her long days.

After passing a few pleasurable hours in her wanderings, or conversing with her friend Emily, she would make her way back to her house where she would make preparations for dinner. In this way, day after day passed with no discernible difference. Each one pleasantly monotonous; with the exception of her rambles, and each one increasingly suffocating. The confines of the house seemed to close in around her as she matured from a school girl into a young woman and her need for new experiences deepened to a point which could not be satisfied with a ramble around the town. Chloe realized that although she may not have an exact destination, she needed to move on or stay trapped just as she was, frozen, with a fate although not terrible, not what she wanted. She stayed in this undecided state for quite a while, several years in fact. Not knowing quite where to go, yet always determined that when the time was right she would make her move.

One afternoon, when the winds blew harshly with a November chill that seemed to reach right inside of her and yank at her, crumbling her resolves and leaving her as bleak as the sky, Chloe was tidying up the already neat house when she spotted an old newspaper lying crumpled under her desk. She smoothed it out, finding the ink had faded and smudged but still able to see that it must have been from one of the passengers who stopped to stretch their legs in the tiny train station. From time to time they would leave a newspaper discarded. Chloe savored these tidbits showing a completely different life style. This newspaper, she saw, was from New York, that magical sounding city which lay by wide expanses of sea, across which, Chloe dared not even imagine, stood the grand cities of Europe. She glanced at it, noting it was dated some time ago before suddenly catching sight of a small bit smeared but still visible which advertised employment opportunities for young women. The description of the employment was torn off but there was enough for Chloe to feel that this had been the push she needed. She now knew that she would go to New York, she would find employment of some kind and be free to exercise her own imagination and to maybe, one day, share her love of writing. Chloe felt as though a fire had been lit inside of her and in that moment determined that before the year was out she would be on the train which made its shrill whistle echo through the town each day.

Chloe counted up her savings. Though not extravagant, her father was a fairly generous man, and it was enough for a train ticket and, she hoped, for lodging. She hadn't the slightest notion what kind of adventures lay before her but she plowed ahead with resolution in her heart and prepared for battle with her family. She picked January third as the day she would depart and bought her ticket accordingly. The date seemed to her appropriate as it was a new beginning for the year as well as for her. She packed her few belongings, and any supplies which she had procured since that fateful November day, despite the arguments of her fathers and brothers. She found solace in the face of her tearful sister however; who acknowledged Chloe's spirit was not one to be contained in such a small and stifling society. Her father, who had always seen his late and beloved wife in Chloe, tried with anger and fear to keep her from leaving. Cries of 'You will never amount to anything in the city, you'll be back by spring' echoed in her ears during the weeks preceding her departure making her cheeks burn with a righteous indignation. Her brothers argued in turns, but as they saw she was not to be swayed, wisely fell silent. Some of the kinder ladies who had heard of her departure, whispered from luncheons to church teas, endeavored to warn her about those of 'loose morals' and the 'dangers of city life', suggesting that perhaps one of such delicate nature as Chloe would be better off safe at home under the protection of her father. All of the kind and unkind words alike made Chloe as fiercely determined to make her way successfully in the city as ever before.

Chapter 2

The train ran through the station each day at noon, providing one of the few distractions from the dusty atmosphere of sameness. The few passengers who stepped out of the great rumbling machine just stopped to stretch their legs. They never stayed. They glanced at the small town, with its brick train station, most probably looking like hundreds of other small towns, and went back inside the train to the comfort of their own compartment when the whistle shrilled its departure again, leaving Chloe to wonder at their destination and to imagine she was on board. The day Chloe took the train, her ticket out into the bright wide world, was a cloudless day, cold, with new January winds whipping up the dry frosty dirt and soot on the edges on the tracks and tangling in the heavy skirts of her and her sister. A dull headache and vaguely throbbing heart blurred Chloe's vision and made her stumble as she climbed the steps into the waiting train. She found an empty compartment, piled her belongings in a corner and sat heavily, leaning against her sister Mary. Her father and brothers stood huddled outside. Their one last appeal had fallen on deaf ears and they wisely let Chloe go without as much bitterness as she feared. Presently the whistle announced the departure of the train, and Chloe stood to hug her sister to her, she who had clung to Chloe's skirts as a toddler had become now a lovely young woman. Chloe watched out the streaky window as the train started on its course. With agonizing slowness it jerked away from the station, and Chloe felt her resolution crumble as she looked at her family, but now it was too late. As the train sped up and passed the boundaries of Stuflen, her resolved strengthened again and she knew that she was making the right choice, despite the pain in her heart and unshed tears in her eyes. The train gathered speed and slowly the scenery of flat green fields sped into a blur and it seemed for a moment that Chloe was the stationary one again, but the moment passed as Chloe realized that this time she was not the one left standing on the platform, this time she was the one moving.

The train ride would be a long one. It would take her east to the great bustling city by the sea. Its very name, New York, brought images to Chloe's mind which was fed by the blurred pictures in newspapers, of businesses, independence, and masses of people. It would be as different as one could get from the drab little town in the middle of the fields. The bustling city filled with individuals as different as she, on the edge of the vast blueness signifying even further unknown, was where she would make her way, and open her eyes to a new life. She had often thought of leaving the town in the long years of her girlhood, often yearned for something more and different. Laying in the small bed in her room at night, scribbling in her many journals, she had often dreamed that the train would be the vehicle of her flight, for how else could she leave the town, but she had never imagined the feelings of trepidation and exhilaration that went hand in hand. One the train, Chloe slept for periods of time, rocked by the steady sway of the great machine she rode. At night she listened to the noises and looked at the darkness out of the window. Sometimes a small cluster of lights would pass by signifying another small town just like hers. She would peer out trying to make out any small detail before it slipped away as so many things had in the years past. She was never able to make out much and presently slipped back into sleep again. She woke to snack on the tidbits that her sister had lovingly wrapped up for her to take, wanting to save her meager savings for New York rather than in the dining car. As she ate, she would gaze out of the streaky windows, dull sunlight sifting through, noting the changing countryside, from farm to field and town and back again. At several points the train stopped its ponderous mass, to take on water or a few passengers. Chloe would step down onto the platform and gaze at the stations, and the surrounding countryside. Much was the same as she had grown up with. In fact it surprised Chloe to see how similar everyone was. It was as if she expected people to be different because she felt so different, so adventurous. She felt as if she ought to look different, however, since no one knew her, a very satisfying feeling indeed, most people gave her a nod and polite smile before passing by intent in their own business. Each time that she stepped back up onto the train and into her compartment she could not hide the glowing feeling inside of her that sang a little song when she realized that she was completely anonymous and that no one was there to tell her what to do. Finally, after hours and hours slipped by so she hardly knew if a day or three had passed, she saw that the fields grew smaller and gave way to towns which became larger and larger until they crowded so close as to have no end, and then the buildings grew tall like trees.

Finally she had arrived. The train station was a huge bustling cavernous place. As different from the station from where she had departed as night was from day. The noise of men, women and children, crying babies and porters deafened her when it echoed on the hard surfaces. Chloe climbed out of the train and made her way toward the entrance where she simply stopped to behold all of the noise and bustling. She took in as much as she could, having plunked right down on her trunk in the middle of the crowds. People pushing past her took no notice of a small young woman all alone in the middle of the station. She felt the gleeful little song burst into a chorus as she gazed in awe at the scene and the city which lay beyond. It was all so refreshing to Chloe, the anonymity, the lack of nosy townspeople, the fact that no one cared who Chloe was nor why she was all alone in a huge big city or where she was going, which was a question that was pressing on Chloe this very moment. With that thought, Chloe hefted the small bag and her trunk and stepped through the wide double doors, squinting at the bright cold sunlight which was no dimmer because of the buildings on either side of the wide street. She had made it here at last and the rest would now depend on her own strengths and innovation.

Chapter 3

New York City; exciting and different; offered many opportunities for both enjoyment and employment. Not that Chloe had time or money for entertainment. Her first step in the city, besides gazing wondrously around in every direction until she felt like a weather vane, was to find a room suitable to stay in. After snatching up a stray newspaper on the floor of the station as she was leaving, she and the paper made their way up the street to a relatively quiet corner. The streets were filled with busy pedestrians and some automobiles as well, sharing the roads with the horses and carts. Not far off she could hear the rumble of another train. She walked several streets before resting her tired arms. Although her trunk was not large, it had a way of seeming to multiply its weight with each street. She found herself in an area of busy stores and other businesses, neatly kept front steps and flower pots in windows of upstairs apartments. The markets lined the ground floor of the buildings on either side of the street providing colorful wares for her to explore at a later date.

A small sign in a window of a barber shop with a bright blue door. She went in and inquired about the room to be rented and was overjoyed to find that it was available. The kindly motherly lady who occupied the top floor of the building had an extra room, and as she had been widowed recently, needed to make an additional income. Her brother owned the barber shop on the ground floor and lived on the second floor with his family. Chloe was delighted with the small room and its one large window looking over the bustling street. As it turned out, her landlady was of the talkative kind and Chloe had only to utter the right phrase in order to find out all sorts of useful information. The bustling street she was on was called Bleecker Street, and there was, in fact, an elevated train not 5 blocks away, and that led to even more opportunities for employment. Chloe saw the numerous shops and offices and banks, but those did not interest her, unless she found nothing else. The larger part of her mind prudently said she should find a type of employment with one of those stores or banks or offices, but then there was that small part which stubbornly insisted on trying to find something more interesting, something where she could hone and use her literary skills. With her small savings, Chloe was able to take a bit of time and seek out employment more to her taste. Although that prudent part of her kept popping up with warnings, she firmly decided to look at the offices and banks and domestic engagements only if no other employment presented itself. Therefore she rode the train daily and wandered streets becoming very familiar with the city. Finally Chloe was able to present her bits of writing at a small but flourishing literary magazine, and, convincing the manager that she was not unused to hard work, she procured a position in the magazine of assistant clerk, or office girl, as she would be more commonly known. The position itself had little to do with the writing that she loved, but it was far more than Chloe had dreamed. Indeed it was ,far more than most young women of her age could hope for in terms of employment.

     Naturally diffident, Chloe found the professionalism of so many more experienced in years and wisdom daunting, but the industriousness and individualism of her colleagues gave her a sense of belonging. Quiet though she was, Chloe had an inner core of strength and she never let new experiences stop her from going where she wanted. The magazine was just the spot for her, the smell of ink her ambrosia. All she needed in the morning was to gaze out of the window of her small room at the top of the house at the dawning day in the city street below, already so busy with carts and peddlers, yelling greetings and shouting at the small urchins who invariably were underfoot. These first days past quickly and pleasantly, as smoothly as the pearls on her mother's necklace, hidden in a sock at the bottom of her trunk. She treasured the days and at night wrote about her experiences with as much detail as possible. Each day she rushed to and fro, carrying, delivering and in general making herself available to the writers who worked with her. It was tiring work but the knowledge and experience she was gaining was invaluable.

Chloe drew a small circle of friends, both in and out of the office building, finding people with her own likes and dislikes, and she cradled the friendships as a mother would her newborn babe. James was an apprentice at the magazine with her. Their friendship had kindled after a completely ordinary accident. He had started at the magazine not a year before she had. Less than a month after she started working, on a blustery cold day in late February, she was hurrying into the office which was almost directly across from her stop on the elevated train. As the wind whipped up her skirts and made the soot and dust blow in endless whirlwinds, her hat, which had served her well in Stuflen, was blown completely from her head in a particularly strong gust. The hat was not a particularly warm one, nor was it very fashionable, but it was the only hat which Chloe possessed. She made a dash across the street in an effort to catch it. Coming from rather a small and old fashioned farm town, she was still unused to the speed with which automobiles turned corners. She didn't quite see the one now bearing down on her as she stepped heedlessly into the road after her wayward hat. Hoisting her heavy wool skirt with one hand, she stretched out the other, just reaching the hat which had been blown across the street right in front of the building which housed the magazine. As soon as she felt its brim, a deafening blast sounded almost on top of her and she was yanked to the curb by a strong arm as the automobile swerved and sped on its way, the driver shaking his head and yelling inarticulately. Chloe turned around to thank her savior to find herself face to face with one of the young men from her magazine. He was glaring at her crossly as he brushed off the now quite dented hat. She started to make a polite thank you but was interrupted loudly.

"What do you think you were doing crossing the road in front of that mad man, you could have been run over! This... thing." He shook the limp hat at her, "Isn't worth it, you know." He handed her the hat which she took, stunned at his outburst, and stalked into the office. Chloe was never one to look for confrontation, but this rude young man had gone too far.

"Excuse me!" Chloe hurried after him and stalled him with a tap on the elbow. "Thank you for your assistance, *sir,* but really, my welfare is none of your concern. Nor is my hat's." With that being said she tucked her poor offended hat in her arm and flounced down the hall to hang up her coat. He followed once he realized she worked in the same office that he did.

"Very well." He held up his hands in mock contrition, "I promise solemnly never to save you or your hat from an oncoming vehicle." At that he laughed, his grin so reminding Chloe of a shamefaced schoolboy that she forgave his rudeness on the spot and decided that they should become friends. She instantly changed her expression and introduced herself.

"I should have seen the car, I have only arrived in New York City just this January and we, in our rural town, are unused to such speed. My name is Chloe Walters. May I ask yours?" At this she held out her hand.

James smiled down at her and told her his name was James Baker. "I did not realize that you worked here or I would not have reacted with such force. To tell you the truth I did think that man was going to run you down. I'm awfully glad he didn't." Chloe found that his eyes, as he gazed at her intently, were a deep blue; and for some odd reason elicited a blush in Chloe's cheeks which she could not explain.

After such an incongruous meeting, the two became quite inseparable, finding such strong similarities in each other. James' ambition was to become a journalist, and the magazine proved to be an adequate stepping stone for him. He was similar in age, talented yet also as inexperienced as she in the literary world. He had grown up in New York however, and was as knowledgeable as she was naïve about the city teeming with different cultures. Chloe enjoyed their literary conversations and looked forward to each morning when his cheery countenance greeted her from his cubby hole at the magazine. Still thinking of herself as much too inexperienced for such thoughts, Chloe knew that a tender and golden friendship was growing, but also knew she needed and desired a lot more than just a post as an assistant in a magazine. However much she valued her independence, every time she saw him, her heart gave an odd little thump. His eyes were the brilliant deep blue of the sea, and she felt like he could look straight into her heart. She wasn't quite sure what to do about that.

Fiona, who completed the small tight knit circle, worked at the market on the corner of Chloe's street, which Chloe frequented on an almost daily basis to buy her simple needs. Chloe found in Fiona a markedly different personality than either her or James, but her lighthearted banter and generous spirit complimented their every gathering. Fiona introduced Chloe to a lovely little park that Chloe was quite unaware of. Chloe mentioned one day as she bought some supplies for her room that she had taken to exploring the city after her day's work was done. With the weather naturally still quite blustery she hadn't much chance to do as much as she hoped.

"Oh, I simply must show you the prettiest little park not far from here. It is not very big, nor even is it an official park, but it's peaceful and pretty. Well, except right now with the slush and mud." Fiona's pretty face crinkled at the messy weather. "Tomorrow come by the shop and we will go out for a ramble. Oh please, it would be such a fun thing to do and get to know one another." Chloe smiled at such an open spirit as Fiona and promised to show up at the duly appointed hour for their "ramble". From this time, the little park became a favorite haunt of theirs and the two very different girls became close friends. It did not take long to move from chatting over sandwiches at the magazine to including James in their almost nightly walks in the small park which had been eked out of a vacant lot a few streets over. The roar of the 6th avenue Elevated train added to the nightly chorus of street traffic. Chloe introduced James tentatively to Fiona, nervously hoping the two would find common tastes, and was immensely relieved to find that Fiona was as warm with him as with her. This mattered hugely to Chloe, for although she had acquaintances and occasional close friends in Stuflen, she had not had the good fortune to experience the closeness that a group could provide. The three friends began to spend all of their time together, what little of it there was, between Fiona helping at her family market and Chloe and James's long days. The lovely Washington Square Park with its grand stone arch did interest them, but as it was a farther walk, they generally took a picnic hamper to the little park in the middle of Christopher Street, next to a dignified church and quiet church yard. That was a three block walk and cold or warm the three friends could be seen there, gay laughter filling the air. Chloe and James frequently read aloud from their own magazine or others like it, each trying to gain a foothold in the literary world while still on the outskirts. Fiona listened while happily turning the pages of her own more lighthearted magazines or newspapers that she always brought from the market, occasionally pointing out a snippet of news or advertisement to Chloe. From their vantage point they were able to see all walks of life pass the church and park.

That first year in the city seemed to be over so quickly, yet Chloe would never forget the feelings of excitement and fear that greeted her at first, and she could never forget the belonging and happiness she gained in later months. It had truly been a wonderful year for Chloe, yet she began to feel the urge for new horizons, a yearning for new and different experiences. Her heart had opened so much during that one year, yet to Chloe, she still looked through her window wondering if she would ever find the peace of being satisfied with what she had.

Chapter 4

The magazine in which Chloe worked was indeed a small one, but even in the lowly position that Chloe held she felt an inescapable growth in knowledge and confidence. She felt ready to take on yet another challenge in her life. No longer was she quite the intimidated and diffident girl as of yore, scurrying to please her employer. The city had kept its promises, had widened her horizons ever so much. Chloe pondered endlessly upon her feelings and need for more fulfillment. She wondered why she felt this way, was she unhappy in the city? Chloe knew she wasn't. The past year had been the happiest year ever, so why was she yearning to expand? She concluded that she simply had to fill her mind with more experiences. She hoped it did not mean that she would be doomed to search endlessly for a peace that never would exist for her. Fiona did not understand these feelings at first. She, already settled down to work in the family store, thinking about her future and a certain brown haired young man, could not understand the need to see different places and expand on what the mind had already grasped. James, on the other hand, did understand. Perhaps the creativity of a writer's mind allowed for such a thing as wanting to feel new experiences. He was saddened to a deep degree to find that Chloe felt this way. He did not like to think about her leaving the city, leaving behind this friendship that had grown so close. He was unable, or unwilling to define his own feelings on the matter, but the prospect of not seeing Chloe on a daily basis was not something he liked to dwell on. This being said, however her friends naturally supported her, and although it was not unimaginable, it was quite improbable that she would depart the city which had so quickly become her home. Chloe kept her eyes and ears open for new opportunities. Just the thought that there were such a variety of experiences out there just beyond her grasp was enough to keep Chloe's nomadic streak in check. Perhaps, hoped her friends, after months of looking in the distance, Chloe would see what was right in front of her and settle down her life in the city that seemed to embrace her at first sight.

    Winter night's harsh cold faded into mild spring evenings, and Chloe, as she sat by her window on so many nights, when the weather was too cold for the park, saw the gradual shedding of garments, which followed the season like a calendar. The wool coats, hats and muffs turned into brighter frocks, lighter skirts and cotton adorning most of the women who lived and worked in this part of the city. The hurried steps of passersby trying to find the quickest way through the cold was replaced by laughter and lingering in the warm spring air. Laden now with more belongings than on her initial trip to New York, and with memories thick as the clouds which covered the city on stormy days, Chloe grew hesitant at the thought of ripping up these tender roots that she had planted. Chloe thought that perhaps her needs could be satisfied with a change in employment more than in location. She craved more challenges, and had so well mastered her duties at the magazine; it was no longer as exciting as before. The thought of travelling did entice her however and from her first, and only, long journey left her with an undeniable thirst for new vistas. All of these thoughts whirled around in her mind one unusually hot evening in late spring, with Fiona.

Chloe was occupied in one of her favorite activities, gazing out of her bedroom window into the darkening street below. After a year and a half in the city, this view never failed to fascinate Chloe. It was quiet in the street below, empty of some of the usual peddlers, having gone home in the heat of the day since there were few pedestrians to linger in the heat. Fiona leafed through one of her favorite newspapers, occasionally reading an excerpt of some sensational headline or another. The two girls passed the evening with the happy boredom of youth when it has too much time in which to think. One small advertisement in particular hidden almost at the very bottom of the last page attracted Fiona's attention, and knowing of her good friend's yearning for challenge and excitement called Chloe over from her window perch.

"Chloe, come look, look at this advertisement."

Chloe roused herself, shaking the wrinkles from her skirt which stuck to her skin in the heat of the day. She peered over Fiona's shoulder as she lay on her stomach on Chloe's bed. The advertisement read quite simply. "Literary assistant needed with experience for one year period. Travel may be required." There was no other explanation, no more words other than a street address in smaller letters below, but it was enough to give Chloe a sparkle in her eye which could not be diminished by Fiona's stern look and advice not to "get her hopes up." She immediately hastened to scribble the address on a crumpled slip of paper that lay upon the table which served as her desk. Promising herself she would go the very next day, as there was no telling when the advertisement first appeared, she resisted the kind offer from Fiona to accompany her in what was surely a fool's errand. Chloe could hardly believe that this opportunity was not hers for the taking, even if Fiona was skeptical but supportive. It seemed that it had been placed in this newspaper just for her eyes, and it was the answer to her heart's desire.

"Are you going to tell James then?" Fiona asked shrewdly, seeing far more than Chloe or James suspected of each other's feelings.

"No. Not right now. I'll go tomorrow midday. There really is not any use in worrying him now. Besides, he has other things on his mind.

"I'm sure he does." Fiona said demurely but with an impish light in her eyes which Chloe, eagerly scanning the newspaper again, did not see.

Chapter 5

After bidding a quick greeting to her friend the following morning as she walked past Fiona's family's market, the only thing, Chloe found, that she could think about was the impending appointment she intended to have with the author of the newspaper advertisement. There had been no other instructions other than the street address on 64th street, a much more affluent part of the city than Chloe was used to. Nevertheless, she was vaguely familiar with the grand residential homes presiding over avenues which were cleaner and not quite as full of vendors. She and Fiona had taken several rambles there during the spring months. She was fairly sure she would have little trouble finding the place. True to her word, she had not informed James of the impending interview nor why she was leaving early. To her relief he was not in his cubbyhole desk when she passed in the morning, and though she missed seeing his warm smile and felt a disappointment which had nothing to do with the interview, it was easier not to have to explain. Most days James was actively pursuing other employment opportunities outside of working hours and spent much of his time either proofreading articles for their magazine or writing small articles and trying to get other newspapers to use them. It was slow work but he had been successful in a small way. She started out in mid-afternoon with the hot sun directly above, glad of her aged but good quality hat she had taken care to remember. She took the elevated train up eight stops to the 58th street terminal, and from there it was not too much farther. Nevertheless she found herself feeling uncomfortably warm in her newest skirt and blouse, looking around the wider streets, lined with more trees than in her area of the city. The door that Chloe made her way toward was freshly painted, as all the other doors were, in a subdued maroon with a discreet brass knocker affixed to the front. She barely noticed more than the location of the house, so great was her trepidation and anticipation at the prospect of perhaps stepping foot into another unknown territory.

      The room that she entered, as bidden by the maid who answered the door, was elegantly appointed. Its thick curtains filtered out any noise from the street. It was lavishly decorated, perhaps in a style somewhat outdated, yet still exuding sophistication. There were two young men and one young lady already present in the room uneasily looking at one another with the knowledge that they were all there for the same reason. Indeed Chloe felt the same unease, and her trepidation increased tenfold as she noted the keen intelligence shining out of the eyes of her fellow interviewees and the smarter and newer clothing as compared to her homely and serviceable wear. Chloe felt distinctly at a loss. One by one the other potential literary assistants were called forward by the maid, and disappeared through a door at the far end of the room. Chloe was left to herself as the last one vanished. Chloe glanced around the room, not really seeing it, and she clenched and unclenched her fingers nervously around her small satchel. She counted the tocks on the tall clock in the hall until she saw the last young man emerge from the room and leave, with a nod of acknowledgement for her.

Finally Chloe was motioned forward to enter the door leading, she surmised, to the interview. Here she almost froze, so astonished was she at the change in appearance of this room to the outer parlor and hall that she stood looking for all the world like some awkwardly placed statue. The entire room, library was what she correctly named it, was out of another time and place. The style was completely different from the distinguished yet outdated opulence of the parlor. The library created such an air of cleanliness and light that it hardly felt like it belonged in a house in the middle of a city. What little furniture that was in the room was of a clean almost severe design, and no sign of the inevitable bric-a-brac and dust catchers. With all of the bookshelves, one would have expected the library to be dark, yet the many windows, including the large bow window which faced a small garden, made the library seem almost surrounded by nature. A very elegant and simple oriental rug covered the honey toned floor. The room spoke of a very individual taste which can only be indulged with means well above what Chloe was used to, even in her prosperous childhood home. A single desk graced the room along with two simply upholstered chairs and a small table. Behind the desk sat probably the most powerful elderly lady that Chloe had ever met. There had been some stalwart old ladies in Chloe's hometown who probably would have faced an entire fleet without blinking an eye, but even they would have quailed in the steely presence of this austere woman.

She collected herself enough to hear the maid announce "Miss Walters", and propelled herself forward into the room. The diminutive maid bid Chloe to sit in one of the chairs facing the desk and left her alone in that intimidating presence. Her unease grew as she was quietly and minutely regarded by the old lady behind the desk. Chloe readjusted her grasp on the reticule containing a few of her writing samples from her personal journals plus a small piece she wrote just last night, which lay inside to be presented for approval like so many children in front of a nanny. She waited for the interview to begin, at least the verbal one. Chloe felt that it already had started as she felt such scrutiny upon entering the room. While she sat, trying not to fidget under the powerful gaze, Chloe did some assessing of her own. The lady, who had been announced as 'The Honorable Mrs. Mainthswaite', was indeed elderly, but very well preserved, traces of considerable beauty clearly visible in the set of her brow and line of her cheekbone. Her dress was simple, yet elegant. The material was most expensive looking and the lace of the blouse made by expert hands. Her steely gray eyes glinted behind her spectacles and shone with an intelligence as great as her former beauty must have been. Clearly she had been a formidable woman in her day and remained so.

The woman motioned for Chloe to hand over any writing samples she may have brought. Quickly and under the stern eye of Mrs. Mainthswaite, Chloe hastened to do as she was bid so as not to incur disappointment. Mrs. Mainthswaite made a small noise of satisfaction upon receiving such papers and Chloe breathed a small sigh of relief. Thus far all seemed well.

Mrs. Mainthswaite read the pages closely as Chloe looked on hiding her anxious expression as best she could. "You seem to put your ideas forth adequately. Good expression, good description. Not too flowery. "Mrs.

Mainthswaite looked over the top of her glasses and added, "You could use a bit more experience couldn't you?"

"Yes Ma'am"

I see the magazine where you are employed is certainly not providing much. And you will have to do away with that deferential air. I already have a good maid, I do not need another. I suppose you have a first name Miss Walters?

"It's Chloe... ma'am." was stammered out by a much intimidated young girl, but the venerable woman had dismissed Chloe as easily as one would a novelty no longer of interest and concentrated again on the pages set in front of her. Those paltry pages which were gathered from the small and limited life experience Chloe had gathered in her twenty-two years on this earth. Chloe thought it better not to interrupt such concentrated on trying to make herself invisible. She was not aware that Mrs. Mainthswaite was quite impressed with Chloe's spirit, and innovation as well as her independence.

"She's got talent ...and potential. Quite a backward upbringing, utterly conventional." Mrs. Mainthswaite muttered these comments to herself as Chloe hovered uncertainly on the edge of her chair, not quite sure if she had been accepted as an adequate secretary to the apparently well-travelled and experienced Mrs. Mainthswaite.

Mrs. Mainthswaite looked up, almost surprised to see Chloe still in her chair. "Well girl, what are you waiting for, get going now, ah yes, you may tell your employer you have another post. One moment" Mrs. Mainthswaite arrested Chloe's movement with a wave of her hand. She took out some heavy stationary and scrawled an elegant note; folded the signed missive and placed it in an envelope which she handed to Chloe. "You may give your employer this; I am aware of his magazine and find it to be an exemplary one. Take care to be here tomorrow at nine o'clock sharp." With that Mrs. Mainthswaite inclined her beautifully shaped silver head and stalked from the room after ringing the bell for the diminutive maid, leaving Chloe breathless and exhilarated.

    Chloe barely felt the hot pavement below her feet as she raced along, heart beating at the tremendous opportunity presented to her in such abrupt fashion. She made her way to the offices of the small magazine that had been like a second home to her during this year and a half in the city that was like a savior from a life of dull complacency. Regret was expressed at her resignation, but hardly surprise, that is, until she thrust the letter from Mrs. Mainthswaite on the desk of her employer. After all office girls do not usually walk into such grand appointments with well-known and highly respected individuals like Mrs. Mainthswaite. Of course being only an office girl, not many people were aware of her flowering skill with pen and paper. With this task done, and noting that James was still not to be seen, Chloe went back to her small room looking out onto the hot street below, not unpleasant in its plainness because it left Chloe with blank walls to dream her own sweet and special dreams of the future. She straightened her room in the desultory manner of someone whose thoughts are occupied with far more important matters and looked at her meager wardrobe critically. It contained mostly clothes from her past life. The life she led in the dusty small Stuflen, to which she bore no ill will After all, it did allow her to escape. Mostly plain skirts and blouses in neutral colors peeked at her, drab but appropriate for work days.

Chloe had squeezed the most out of her small income, which was used mostly for food and board, and purchased some nice fabrics. Her kind landlady had let her use her sewing machine to make a few new outfits, such as the one she was wearing today. She had splurged on some bits of lace to dress up the collars of a few blouses. She wished she could afford to make a nice dress or two or even buy one of the beautiful ones displayed in the store windows but for now she would be happy with what she had.

That night, the three friends met in their favorite spot for a picnic dinner, the night air being much cooler and fresher than the hot air still trapped indoors from the day. Chloe broke the news to James about her interview with a little hesitation. He had not even known about the advertisement. She wasn't sure how he would feel, and truth be told, she wasn't even sure she wanted to explore her own feelings about leaving either. Most of her was intensely excited about the opportunity; however the small part which got goose bumps whenever he looked over at her was very sad. James was amazed and supportive, although he too looked sad at the prospect of her leaving the magazine.

"A Mrs. Mainthswaite?" James's eyebrows rose incredulously and then he laughed at her ignorance of the name. Chills shot through Chloe at his laugh. Since Chloe had only been in the city a year and a half, her knowledge of society was almost nonexistent. Since she had no means nor with to enter society, she had no knowledge of the names of leading families such as the Mainthswaite's. "Yes I know the name well" James said in response to Chloe's unasked query. "She is a wealthy widow; her husband had been one of the chief benefactors in the publication of many literary magazines in the city. I also believe he was involved to some extend in some of the newspapers, although to what extend I do not know. Mrs. Mainthswaite has continued in his footsteps, perhaps showing more intelligence than her husband, and is surely more formidable than he. She keeps a tight rein on her employees and is rumored to have a most acerbic tongue.

Chloe considered what he said and found that it was in keeping with the impression she had gained in meeting Mrs. Mainthswaite.

"She is also supposed be one of the most influential ladies in fashion." Fiona chimed in, "Well, for her age."

"She certainly spoke her mind," said Chloe in her soft well-modulated accent, which was in keeping with a slower sort of lifestyle than one could fine in the city. Chloe found that it wasn't too much of an effort to speak well of people and usually tried to keep her opinions to herself until she gained a greater depth of knowledge of the person or circumstance in question. "I found her to be a most intelligent person and indeed did also have a beautifully appointed house." Chloe remembered the wonderful airy library with its thick rug and simple graceful furniture with shelves and shelves of books which Chloe longed to read.

"Secretary and who knows what lay beyond with such an employer?" James spoke wistfully at the thoughts that arose in his mind, for he and Chloe shared many of the same desires, one being to gain experience and connect with others with the same literary aspirations, and another as of yet unspoken but very much a part of each other's minds.

Especially in that pleasant moment before falling asleep and finding that the other filled such a large part of their thoughts. James saw the sideways glances from Chloe when she thought he wasn't looking, and he was coming to realize perhaps they felt the same way about one another. However he also was trying his best to make a name for himself as a journalist, and knew that he needed to find his way first.

Chloe's mind was on the practicalities of the new post. "I haven't received a clue as to what I shall be doing but I imagine it will be to assist Mrs. Mainthswaite in some aspect, perhaps her knowledge of publishing will help me in the future. Of course I am merely speculating since I do not know anything more than I did before the interview."

Fiona provided some sage advice for Chloe, which she would have been remiss not to heed. Fiona pointed out that Chloe needed to keep her feet on the ground and that her thinking too far ahead was a bit presumptuous, as no one knew, except for the honorable Mrs. Mainthswaite, when or where Chloe's duties would take her. Chloe hoped that the travelling as specified in the advertisement would be quite as interesting as she fantasized and she looked forward to new vistas and greater experiences, but she found that whenever she happened to glance toward James, his piercing blue eyes were regarding her with an indefinable expression, which flustered Chloe more than she would ever care to admit.

"Yes indeed" stammered Chloe feeling a warmth creep into her cheeks. She was most grateful for the deepening dusk as it hid her surely noticeable flush. "Of course I should keep my attention on the present."

Thus reassured by her stalwart friends and pressed upon to make sure to keep them apprised of any new developments, she laughed delighted in the honesty and warmth of their friendship and reminded them that she was surely still available for as many evening gatherings as the weather permitted.

Chapter 6

    The next morning dawned hot and sultry again, the sun making a reluctant entrance as if it grew tired of doing battle with the hazy clouds. The refreshing breeze of the previous evening had dissipated. The threat of rain was imminent and indeed the tingle of atmosphere could forecast storms for the afternoon. Streaks of soot clung to the window in spots ad made the pale light seem to appear even more pathetic. Chloe was already wide awake, had been in fact long before the sun made its desultory appearance. Her excitement and nervousness mounted as she surveyed her wardrobe and selected one of her newer skirts. The skirt she chose was a green one with a pleasing scoop to the neck of her blouse. The fabric was light enough to withstand the muggy late spring heat. She took a last glance out of her window and began to dress her honey toned hair simply but with care, and prepare herself for the walk and first step into a brand new adventure. As she let herself out of the front door into a street bustling with activity, she briefly thought about how much easy she navigated the city with its crowds. How different she had become from just two winters ago when she stood on the brink of her first adventure, in a tiny and stagnant town. She became aware of a familiar figure sitting on the front stoop.

"James, what are you doing here at this hour?" Chloe exclaimed, unable to keep the evident pleasure from her voice and most likely her face as well.

"I thought you could use some company on such a memorable occasion." James casually fell into step with Chloe as they expertly dodged busy peddlers and errand boys on the street. Chloe reflected on how much ease there was between her and James and the simple joy of walking down the street at his side. She glanced sideways and found him smiling to himself in much the same manner.

"That is most kind." Chloe murmured her thanks. "And what plans do you have for the day?"

"I was asked to edit two short stories that Mr. Selby wants to publish for next month's edition" said James as he stood back and motioned her to precede him onto the platform to wait for her train. "I have also written an editorial which I shall try to submit to the Times."

"How wonderful James. I am sure they will accept your editorial. Any quality newspaper would be lucky to have your editorial." Chloe was happy for James, and for herself. It seemed that they both were having wonderful luck pursuing their dreams in the literary world.

As they rode the elevated train nearer her destination, Chloe fell silent as she contemplated more and more the duties that would be hers upon arrival at Mrs. Mainthswaite's home. Not half an hour later they turned into the shady street, gracious with its wrought iron and freshly painted doors. The camaraderie that had been constant during the ride fell off as Chloe and James felt the uncomfortable awkwardness of saying a lighthearted goodbye when neither of them was feeling very lighthearted. James removed his hat, fidgeted for a minute and put a tentative hand on Chloe's arm, then seemed to think better of it and backed off a few feet for a more formal goodbye. Chloe felt relieved. Darting for the door with a hurried "see you tonight with Fiona", she was unable to quench the burning feeling in her cheeks.

Chloe rang the bell and was gratified to have the petite maid from yesterday answer quite quickly and usher her into the parlor, as she was very much aware of a pair of piercing blue eyes burning into her back. The quiet closed around her and she felt the hush of age and of quality surround and ease the tightness in her shoulders. Whatever happened, she was here now. Today of course, Chloe was the only one in the parlor since everyone had been politely turned away. The maid turned to her, a trim girl in lace uniform and cap, no more than sixteen, and bid her to sit.

"My name is Grace Ma'am. Mrs. Mainthswaite will be down directly. Please be comfortable." With that Grace inclined her head pertly and left the room. Chloe noticed that Grace had unusually fine diction for a girl of her age and station. She wondered if perhaps Grace's employer had educated her. Clearly Mrs. Mainthswaite was a woman who would not tolerate slovenliness or stupidity. Chloe sat for no more than ten minutes in the quiet of the parlor with only the ticking clock for company. She contemplated how this day would unfold and whether it would eventually yield avenues to faraway places and grand opportunities, as she idly gazed at the bright green leaves of late spring moving past the broad windows. There was a lazy hot breeze this morning, sluggish in the humidity and it looked as if the trees were in need of some pruning. A few well-dressed children walked sedately by with a nanny pushing a baby carriage.

The door at the back of the room, from the library, opened and Mrs. Mainthswaite stepped briskly through, dressed impeccably, far simpler than society dictated but fitting to her personality. Her tailored skirt was very plain but with a richness that spoke of undeniable quality. She seemed to favor a dark almost silvery gray blouse which draped in quiet dignity on her slender frame. It was easy to believe that she was a fashion leader in her circles.

"Good morning Chloe. I commend your punctuality." Chloe caught a hint of an accent in the austere voice of Mrs. Mainthswaite but it was very faint. "I will outline your duties presently and we shall commence your work. Perhaps you would find a cup of tea or coffee favorable?" Before Chloe could stammer a reply, Mrs. Mainthswaite reached for the bell to summon little Grace again.

Grace appeared swiftly, bringing to mind a sprite or fairy in one of Chloe's childhood tales. She took Mrs. Mainthswaite's instructions calmly, gave a brief bob and disappeared into the nether regions of the house, which were, of course, still mysterious and forbidding to Chloe.

While waiting for the refreshments, Mrs. Mainthswaite explained to Chloe that she was in need of a good secretary to organize her substantial amount of notes and correspondence dealing with her life, influential family and her late husband. Her goal was to leave a fairly clear and detailed set of memoirs for her descendants and others interested in the vast amount of knowledge she had gained in and out of the publishing world. Her extensive travels had left her with an admirable knowledge of the world. She planned on traveling to Europe in the next year to settle some business abroad as her family had some property holdings in England and France. During her travels she would require a companion, intelligent enough to take any notes and letters that may be required.

"Well, girl, do you think you can handle the duties I have outlined?" Mrs. Mainthswaite demanded with customary brusqueness. Chloe, intimidated by this stern manner during the first interview of yesterday was beginning to see that it was merely Mrs. Mainthswaite's no nonsense attitude. She admired the older lady for her ability to push aside niceties in order to deal with the business at hand and began to feel more comfortable in her answers. Chloe assented eagerly, having heard the assignment which sounded ever so interesting and as the two spoke, Chloe's confidence returned and gave her more strength to relate to this woman of incredible personality. Presently Grace entered again bearing a tray with a silver coffee pot and china cups, along with a plate of dainty sweet pastry. Chloe was quite happy to partake of these, as she had not eaten anything in the morning, being too nervous and afraid to burden her quaking stomach with food. Mrs. Mainthswaite applied her steely glare to Chloe once again and began an interrogation of sorts into the background, experiences and insights Chloe had gathered throughout her young life. Most girls of twenty-two were already settled into domestic bliss.

When Mrs. Mainthswaite asked Chloe why she had chosen this path rather than stay in the safe comfortable and stifling confines of her father's house, Chloe felt herself at last able to speak freely about her views on this point. Chloe had always felt that there was more to be experienced from life other than what she considered to be drudgery. Her childhood had been one of chores and housework, keeping house for her father and brothers and looking after her sister. Having only vague memories of her own mother, Chloe had not seen the happiness that her mother had gained from her house and children. She had never understood that her mother had balanced this domesticity with her own intelligence, needs and wants, or that Chloe's father had always looked upon his wife as a partner not a servant. Chloe ended by saying that she felt that there was much more to be experienced in life and didn't want to be hampered by anyone else's constant demands. As she was ending this bold monologue, Chloe knew that she wasn't being entirely truthful. She knew already that a desire for more than friendship was clouding her judgment, as elusive as that whispered breeze which used to play through the long grasses back home. Never able to be contained, was the image of James' piercing blue eyes which was what she saw every time she closed her eyes. But she did also know that when the time came, if ever, she would meet him equally as a free standing woman, satisfied that her life was full. Chloe flushed at the thoughts which had flashed through her head but said nothing as her new employer noted Chloe's blushing cheeks. Evidently Mrs. Mainthswaite was satisfied and perhaps impressed with Chloe's unexpected verbal unburdening. As a rule, Chloe was not extremely verbal; indeed perhaps the only person who knew most of her desires which lay behind her flight out of Stuflen was James. Under the skilled questioning, and perhaps trustworthy personality of her companion, however, she had unburdened herself of thoughts and memories which she didn't expect to stir. This left Chloe with a clean sort of feeling and it energized her even further.

The remainder of the day passed at an amazing pace. Chloe found herself in the library with her first task of organizing Mrs. Mainthswaite's correspondence chronologically.

"This should be a good start for you. I find it always helps to establish a firm timeline. I have several appointments I must keep; otherwise I would naturally be here to answer any questions, however, in that event, just keep the letter to the side. I thank you." Mrs. Mainthswaite smiled grimly and stalked out of the room.

Chloe was quite nonplussed. Mrs. Mainthswaite smiled so seldom, it took Chloe by surprise. Right then and there she decided to befriend little Grace who seemed to be a nice creature, interestingly educated and tutored in diction and social skills. Chloe felt sure she would also learn more of her employer from Grace.

Chloe immersed herself in the highly interesting correspondence which was housed in two large boxes. It contained details of Mrs. Mainthswaite's life, and of her husband's profession, the publishing ventures and shows how strongly Mrs. Mainthswaite had been involved in the business. Clearly Mrs. Mainthswaite had been much more than a dutiful wife and fashionable hostess to a powerful magnate. Indeed if it had not been for her, the business which had proven so successful would not have been possible. It appeared she also was quite skilled in managing small details of the business and investing money both in and out of the household. In addition to her vast intelligence in the business of publishing, she had a family nearby which Chloe found hard to imagine. A son and his wife and children lived in the city.

At this point, several hours into Chloe's work, Grace came shyly into the room and invited Chloe to the kitchen to partake of some luncheon. Chloe had not realized how hungry she was, so caught up in her work. She agreed with alacrity and followed Grace through a twisting hallway into a bright and airy kitchen with a large scrubbed wooden table. Grace explained that she had eaten already but the cook, who introduced herself as Mrs. Kingston dished up a bowl of soup and gave Chloe a glass of iced tea, since the day was such a warm one.

"Well Chloe, what do you think of our little family here." Mrs. Kingston was a large comfortable looking woman with an ample bosom which was covered in a calico apron. She smiled motherly and winked at Chloe, instantly putting her at ease.

"I like it. Mrs. Mainthswaite is a very interesting person, and this is such a beautiful house." Chloe smiled as she sipped her soup looking around the kitchen and at its gleaming pots hanging from the ceiling. "This soup is delicious Mrs. Kingston. Thank you so much. It beats my ham sandwich I brought along with me." Chloe laughed.

Mrs. Kingston patted Chloe's arm. "Don't you bother yourself with bringing lunch. Half of the time Mrs. Mainthswaite's not even here and we have more than enough to feed a dozen grown men. It'll be nice for me and Grace to have a little company." Mrs. Kingston nodded to Grace who had busied herself washing up some of the dishes. "Grace has been here since she was 12 years old. Mrs. Mainthswaite found her begging downtown with nothing but a thin dress between her and winter. Me and Grace we do all the housework here, not that there is much of it. Mr. Kingston looks after the outside and garden." Chloe nodded, finding this little tidbit about Grace enlightening, and ate the remaining soup while listening to Mrs. Kingston give her some background on the street.

"Thank you so much Mrs. Kingston, I must get back to work, but I enjoyed the company as much as the lunch!"

"Aren't you such a polite little thing? You're not from around then, didn't you say?" Mrs. Kingston took a firm hold of Chloe's arm while escorting her back to the library.

"No ma'am, I grew up in Ohio. I have been here for about a year and a half." Chloe turned at the doorway and gave her a warm smile which she hoped would convey her gratitude at being made to feel so comfortable. After receiving another motherly pat from Mrs. Kingston she proceeded inside and set herself to her work again happy with the knowledge she had gleaned from Mrs. Kingston, and with the fellowship. She worked for some time with only the tick of the clock and occasional street sound. The oppressive heat made even the birds inactive in the sullen afternoon. Four o'clock came with a loud bong of the clock and creak of the door which made Chloe look up with a start. Mrs. Mainthswaite had evidently returned judging by the murmur of conversation. Chloe waited for her and came back to herself feeling like she had spent much of the day in the past. Most of the correspondence and papers were fairly well organized, but time had taken its toll and things had shifted here and there.

Mrs. Mainthswaite appeared in the doorway, back ramrod straight and head held high. "Good afternoon Chloe." Her eyes strayed to the neat piles which Chloe had started organizing and the drawer of empty leather binders which she was planning on filling in order. "Ah you seem to have made an adequate start. I see you have reached a natural stopping point." Mrs. Mainthswaite took a seat in one of the chairs near the desk. "I plan on taking a trip to Europe at some point in the near future. I have not yet determined the exact timeline for this. I wanted to apprise you of the definite possibility since I will require a travelling companion. Please consider this. You make take your leave now and we will commence on the morrow. Good day." Mrs. Mainthswaite stood with an abruptness which signified a dismissal and stalked out the side down back towards the kitchen. Chloe was left to show herself out, with Grace at the door bobbing a curtsy and offering a warm smile. Chloe returned the smile with interest and passed out of the gate to make her way back to the much humbler building that she called home.

Chloe wondered if indeed Mrs. Mainthswaite even liked her. She supposed that when one was of a certain age and social standing, it was unnecessary to observe every social convention. Still it would have been nice to know for sure if she was agreeable to Mrs. Mainthswaite. Apparently, at least, Mrs. Mainthswaite felt confident enough in Chloe's abilities to propose to take her along on a trip to Europe. With this, Chloe's head began to spin with visions of travelling to far off places, and she dreamt of that all the way home, almost missing her stop. Once safely on the ground, she ran all the way to Fiona's where she found her waiting with impatience and curiosity plainly visible on her face.

Fiona was never one to stand on ceremony. "Well?" She demanded before Chloe so much as put on foot on her stoop.

"Well what?" asked Chloe innocently, as she tried unsuccessfully to hide a smirk at the sight of her friend positively dancing with anticipation. Her heart filled with joy that she had such wonderful friends who were so supportive and caring and yet again she felt the love of the city envelope her.

"Really, Chloe, how could you tease? How was it? How was she? What did you do?" Chloe motioned that her friend come outside, and linking her arm through Fiona's, they began to stroll aimlessly down the street. In this way Chloe was able to be silent for a few moments in order to organize her thoughts into a more cohesive unit as they were still scattered from the overwhelming first day of a new job, and the excitement that always accompanies it.

"Well…It was…all that I could have hoped for." Chloe replied, thinking hard to describe her exact feelings upon the completion of her first day. "I was surrounded with knowledge, wisdom, elegance, wealth; Mrs. Mainthswaite is certainly quite a character." She chuckled a bit, thinking about some of the more pointed questions that she had been asked by her new employer that morning. She thought about how brusque the older lady seemed yet how astute in her observations. "She seems to have no need or desire to observe the accepted social etiquette required by society and is very much her own woman. Her intelligence and her independence is most apparent and her thirst for information is as great. I expect that is why she has become such a formidable figure in the literary world. She also has many ties with England which demands her presence there in the near future. She has requested that I accompany her as a travelling companion as well!"

Chloe blushed at this declaration, feeling the excitement pulse through her body as unbidden and vaguely exotic thoughts swept through her mind. Fiona squealed with delight, causing two delivery boys to turn around in alarm. She was as happy as Chloe could have wished at the news. Fiona never grudged her good wishes for Chloe for she knew how hard earned was Chloe's independence and happiness, although she did not share the same desires. Fiona had other thoughts to occupy herself with in a much more domestic way, having grown into a comely young woman who had no other wish than to be happy and blessed with a family. She found Chloe's aspirations difficult to understand at times but understood how their differences made them all the more closer and she rejoiced in Chloe's happiness with a full heart. As the two girls reached Chloe's room, they indulged in an enthusiastic romp in celebration of the new job and the exciting prospects ahead. James appeared in the door way at that moment, quite a bit earlier than usual and caught Chloe and Fiona in the midst of their girlish high spirits. They froze at the sight of him lounging against the open door, unable to hide his amused smile. As always his eyes lingered appreciatively and tenderly on Chloe's face before he hefted himself from his post and joined the girls as they self-consciously straightened their skirts and sat demurely on the bed. Just as eager as Fiona he had rushed through his day in order to find out all the details from Chloe about her first day in Mrs. Mainthswaite's employ. He made Chloe repeat all that she had told Fiona, which she did, omitting the part about the travel plans.

"Well it sounds almost too good to be true Chloe" he exclaimed, pulling the only available chair towards the middle of the room and facing the girls. They had left the door open in deference to Chloe's motherly landlady who did not find it suitable for young women to entertain male guests behind closed doors.

"It was." Chloe agreed. "However Mrs. Mainthswaite isn't the friendliest of people. I really could not make out if she liked me or not."

"My dear Chloe." Chloe always felt herself flush when James dropped these occasional endearments. "If she hadn't liked you, do you think you would be returning tomorrow? Definitely not. Mrs. Mainthswaite is not one to simper. She knows what she wants and expects others to do as she says. He looked at her full in the face and asked seriously, "what about the travel in the advertisement?"

"Oh." Chloe hadn't meant to tell him about that part just yet, forgetting that he had seen the advertisement on her desk. She thought perhaps of waiting until she had more details. Her excitement vanished at the thought of not only seeing the wonderful far off places but at spending quite a bit of time apart from James. Perhaps that was, her mind kept piping up, because James had come to mean much more to her than she pretended, and perhaps she felt that tug on her heart getting stronger, even in the midst of this wonderful opportunity for travel. "Well… Mrs. Mainthswaite did mention that, but had no details at the moment."

"Were you not going to tell me that?" James stood quickly, his arresting blue eyes pinned her down and Chloe felt unable to breathe at his anger. "Does she expect you to trot off after her at a moment's notice?"

"James, I don't know. Why does this bother you?"

"I don't know. I had hoped you would tell me all of your news. You told Fiona." He gestured to Fiona, who was watching the volley of words with alarm.

"I was going to tell you James, I don't have any details yet, so it would have been pointless to… jump ahead of ourselves."

"You're very prudent Chloe. It doesn't become you. Congratulations on your new employment. I would stay and celebrate but I have work to do." With that he gave a half smile to the stunned Fiona, who sat on the bed unmoving. He looked back at Chloe from the threshold, anger softening for a moment. "I'll see you tomorrow."

Fiona and Chloe sat in silence for a moment collecting their thoughts and Fiona burst out "What a child he is."

Chloe said slowly, "I didn't think he would be angry because I neglected to mention that travel was a distinct probability. I don't even have any details."

Fiona looked sympathetically at Chloe and said, "Chloe, it wasn't that you neglected to mention it, it was that you would be travelling at all. Don't you understand?"

Chloe shook her head. "No. Why can't he just be happy for me?"

Fiona sighed. "It's just as well then, he will come back tomorrow. Come; let's go get some fresh air. It's quite stifling in this room." She took Chloe's arm and led her downstairs to walk along the streets this time all the way to Washington Square Park where they could gain some peace and calmness. Fiona was probably the only one of the trio who was satisfied of Chloe and James' feelings for each other, and in an attempt to draw Chloe out of her brooding mood, chattered away lightheartedly about dresses and new styles of hats and the like. Eventually the sky grew darker and as purple streaked across the sky chasing the sun over the horizon and made the city's many lights twinkle brighter than the stars. They headed back home where Chloe could close her eyes against a night which was supposed to be wonderful and happy. She fell asleep on a mood more desolate than she had felt in a long time, and hoped that the morning would dawn on a better day.

The next morning indeed dawned bright and sultry; the sullen threatening air of yesterday having been dissipated only slightly by several early morning thunderstorms. Chloe chose her outfit with care yet not quite as much enthusiasm ate her solitary breakfast and prepared to leave for Mrs. Mainthswaite's house. Yet again, she saw a familiar figure sitting on the stoop as she exited her building; today however an attitude of weariness pervaded him.

"James! You're making this a habit of sorts." Chloe surveyed him, noting signs of fatigue in the eyes she had come to find so dear.

"I wanted to come and apologize for my outburst Chloe. I'm really sorry. I am very happy for your wonderful new position you know." He fell into step beside her as she led the way through the throng of early morning shoppers with their baskets laden with food.

"I know James. I am sorry, I didn't mean to keep any information from you it was just…" She faded away unsure of quite how to continue and well aware of the current that was passing between them as palpable as this morning's thunderstorms.

James took her arm, holding her perhaps a bit closeer than usual as he guided her across the street. "I have to go, but I hope to see both you and Fiona tonight. Perhaps we can have a proper celebration of your good fortune."

She smiled up at him, shielding her eyes from the sun which shone brighter today in the blue sky. "I'd like that a lot. I do hate if there was a constraint between us."

James' expression grew serious and he looked at her closely before nodding in agreement. "I don't either, but if we are going to always be friends, there are bound to be some differences of opinion at times. Our friendship is stronger though."

Chloe nodded at that. Friends, she thought, that was a good word. She thought, she hoped, for more, but right now, with so many things whirling in her head, 'friends' was a very good word. "I have to go, that's the train approaching. I will see you this evening. I am so glad you came this morning." She clamped her hat upon her head causing James to smirk, remembering the first time they had met, and clattered up the steps to the platform.

Chapter 7

The day passed as quickly as the first, though now armed with a certain familiarity, Chloe was much more certain of how her day would unfold. She quickly finished the piles that she had begun so neatly the day before, and was able to arrange neat leather binders in chronological order, which she hoped at least impressed Mrs. Mainthswaite. There was no talk about the preceding day's hint of travel, but Chloe was content with the knowledge that Mrs. Mainthswaite would be more forthcoming when needed. As she worked she emanated a happy glow which was noticed by her employer. Chloe detected a twinkle in the older lady's stern visage, but nothing was said. She enjoyed another delicious lunch prepared by Mrs. Kingston in the kitchen and conversed happily with the motherly cook and Grace about the workings of the house. As the end of the day neared, Mrs. Mainthswaite returned from unknown parts of the house to the library where she had spent some time now and then throughout the day making herself familiar with Chloe's progress. Upon Chloe's timid query, Mrs. Mainthswaite declined the need for Chloe to return on the morrow. As Mrs. Mainthswaite put it that she 'needed her privacy sometimes.' Again she smiled that rusty smile that looked as if it was quite out of practice and bade Chloe a good weekend.

"Mind that you're here Monday morning sharp."

"Yes Mrs. Mainthswaite. Thank you." Chloe murmured and found her way to the kitchen where she could say good evening to Mrs. Kingston and Grace, the former being elbow deep in flour.

"Have a good weekend then dearie. Make sure you watch, it might storm again tomorrow. I can feel it in my knee." Mrs. Kingston spoke with the melancholy satisfaction of a lifelong sufferer.

"Good bye Chloe. See you on Monday." Grace piped up and watched as Chloe let herself out the back door into the hot evening.

The next weeks flew by. Chloe spent some time during the week end in the huge newly opened public library perusing the shelves and filling pages of her journal. Once Mrs. Kingston's well predicted storms had abated, the three friends spent a pleasant evening or two each week strolling down to their little park, or just gathering at Chloe's boardinghouse. Fiona wisely kept the talk on lighthearted subjects. The oppressive heat was back in the city, steaming it in a swath of humidity and haze as June left them. As the weeks progressed, Chloe noticed that Fiona's appearances became increasingly more erratic. Often she caught up with Chloe and James, hurrying after them, and leaving earlier than usual with blushes and downcast glances. Chloe did not have to ask the reason for these behaviors, although she said nothing to James. Many nights had seen the girls giggling over future romances and writing names in the dusty dresser in Chloe's room. One by far had figured often in Fiona's vocabulary. Although Chloe had met Fiona's friend Hank but once, she surmised most correctly that they would be hearing more of him in the near future.

The erratic nature of Fiona's appearances lent an unforeseen and awkward cast to the evening gatherings. With Fiona gone, Chloe felt increasingly tongue tied and uncomfortable in James' company. Their chatter was the same as ever, each sharing their day's experiences and funny incidents which made the day brighter, but now a certain warmth in James' expression and a dull ache in Chloe's heart made their encounters seem more fraught with anxiety. Each breathed a silent sigh of relief when Fiona joined the group because unknown to them, she was certain of the reason for their awkwardness and strove to make each comfortable, enough to perhaps get past their fears and openly admit their feelings, now all too apparent to ignore, for each other. In her own way, Fiona was the shrewdest of all three. James with his journalistic skill and keen ambitions and Chloe with her talents could never have the innate common sense that Fiona possessed. Still the group forged on. Each to his or her own life's journey, but always keeping close contact with each other, for that tie of friendship was most important to each of them. More and more did Chloe find herself drawing closer to her employer, who, despite the caustic exterior, Chloe found to be of like mind with regard to their ideas on writing, current events, and naturally women's rights. Mrs. Mainthswaite, in turn, helped Chloe immensely by allowing her to catch a glimpse of a woman of such strength, individuality and intelligence that Chloe strove to emulate her in every respect. The day to day duties of Chloe's work did not vary from that first full week; however the organizing of Mrs. Mainthswaite's correspondence was far from tedious. After the first month, Chloe felt as comfortable in the employ of Mrs. Mainthswaite as possible. Her talents in writing had become even more evident when Mrs. Mainthswaite had asked her to start a brief outline or her correspondence which she had been previously organizing. Mrs. Mainthswaite was satisfied with her concise style, and though it was not the dreamy and introspective style of Chloe's journals; she adapted quite well and proved once again that she was a valuable asset. Chloe enjoyed her daily lunches in the domain of Mrs. Kingston, and together with Grace, the midday meal was one of laughter and gaiety.

Chapter 8

    The weather had turned slightly cooler, a pleasant change from the hot and sultry June. The July sky was brilliant blue, framed in puffy white clouds. It accented the darkening green of summer foliage. The first Saturday of July, Chloe decided to splurge a little of her meager savings on a new skirt and perhaps a blouse or two. She had Fiona headed up to 6th Avenue to see what they could find. Fiona had an eye for color and a flare for stretching her dollar, so Chloe knew they would find luck.

    "How is your friend Hank doing?" Chloe asked impishly, as they loitered on the sidewalk, enjoying the slight breeze which fluttered their skirts and swirled around their ankles.

    Fiona smiled broadly, her clear wide eyes shining with happiness. "Oh he is fine. Very busy, naturally. He, he's been working hard to save; his uncle wants him to take over his butcher's shop! There is a lovely apartment over the top of it. And it's only six streets up."

    "And has he told your parents that?" Chloe inquired. "You haven't been overly talkative about him in front of me either." She teased.

"Wellll, we haven't exactly talked to my parents yet. But we will. Soon. So I haven't wanted to… jinx it, by saying anything to anyone. Of course they know already, I am sure" Fiona sighed happily and tucked her arm through Chloe's. "What about you and James?" She inquired with raised eyebrow.

"Um, what about us?" Chloe couldn't hide the burning flame rising up to her cheeks. She had always detested the fact that she blushed so easily. Her sister said she wore her emotions for the world to see.

"Oh Chloe, a blind man would notice the way you two look at each other."

"I wasn't aware how obvious it was."

Fiona laughed, "It is indeed. Come, why is it so complicated?"

"It just is." Chloe sighed. "I never expected this. I came to New York to further my career and to, well, I guess to find a place to fit. Not to 'catch a husband' as some of the ladies back home would say."

"Chloe, you can't help how you feel. Not everything can be planned."

"No. I know." Chloe agreed with this, but at the same time she felt that it should not have happened so. Why was it that she had to meet James now when she was at such a very important and transitional step in her life? He intruded in her life almost forcefully, that day when she very nearly was run over. His eyes were what she saw from the first. How they could make her feel as if he was reaching into her mind and soul, she did not know, but it was a familiar and safe and scary feeling all at one time. Chloe knew she would never want to endanger their friendship or other closer feelings they had, but sometimes she wished she could have met him at another time.

"Chloe look at that beautiful suit!" Fiona pointed excitedly to a shop laden with fashionable skirts and suits. The two girls entered the shop and were delighted to find the prices modest. In a short time Chloe had found not only a beautiful suit of light green cotton, with a fashionably tailored look, as well as two blouses with elegant pleats and lace at the collar which would dress up her collection of serviceable skirts at home. They left the shop laden with packages and high spirits.

"You need a new dress Chloe" Fiona declared as they started back to the train.

"Whatever for?" Chloe shook her head. "I have two which I made not six months ago, besides I have no occasion to wear a dress any fancier. Plus this new suit is just gorgeous."

"If you are going to travel anywhere you will need a nice dress. Plus, you never know when you will need one for a wedding." Fiona smiled slyly and although Chloe knew nothing had been made official, the prospect of a wedding for Fiona and Hank hung in the air with tantalizing promise.

"Fiona, I hardly have the funds for a fancy dress now, look how I overspent today."

"Leave it to me, Chloe. All you need is the material. And I have something in mind." Chloe sighed and led the way back home; resigned to finding some material for a fancy dress which she knew would hang in her closet gathering dust, until Fiona's wedding most probably.

Chloe left Fiona at her apartment above the family shop and brought her packages home to lay on her bed and admire. The two blouses were elegant, more stylish than anything she had already and would really look nice with any of her skirts. The suit was a delicate moss green. The skirt was narrow, almost constricting by her standards, and the jacket had lovely lapels and buttons on the cuff. It was Chloe's favorite color, so immediately had caught her eye. Chloe held up the skirt and looked down at her scuffed boots that looked even more worn compared to the new clothes. Although it would be lovely to have some new shoes, right now, Chloe would make do with some shoe polish.

The Monday dawned bright and clear, with a certain delicious crispness in the air that brings a spring in the step. The trees and lawns in Mrs. Mainthswaite's neighborhood were heavy with lush greenery. Chloe smiled to herself as she walked along in her new suit, anticipating an exciting day ahead. Mrs. Mainthswaite had told her that later this coming week she would discuss plans for a trip in the near future. Chloe was still not quite sure how much use she would be to Mrs. Mainthswaite when she could very well remain in the city and finish outlining the vast stores of correspondence that

Mrs. Mainthswaite had amassed over the years. Chloe suspected that Mrs. Mainthswaite was planning on bringing her to Europe primarily for company, as the older lady would be travelling alone otherwise, but Chloe wasn't one to complain, least of all about a chance in a lifetime as this. She looked forward to hearing about the trip, which had no definite date but would be planned for some time in autumn. Additionally, Fiona had asked particularly if she and James would have dinner with her and a ramble in the park Thursday evening. Chloe suspected that this may bring tidings of some importance from Fiona, especially considering their conversation from Saturday. This brought great joy to Chloe, but also a sadness which always accompanies this news, because soon there would be a fourth added to their chummy group. This also meant Fiona would have other commitments and would not be available for as many of their walks in the park or picnic suppers in Chloe's room. Chloe was sure Hank would be a delightful addition to the three, but it would change things. Soon enough Chloe reached the maroon painted door of Mrs. Mainthswaite's and sternly put aside her daydreaming and entered the house as comfortably as if it were her own.

Chapter 9

True to her word, Mrs. Mainthswaite showed Chloe a plan for their "jaunt" to Europe, as she put it. For Mrs. Mainthswaite, it was naturally something to be looked forward to, but not with the wonder of a new traveler. She was so familiar with the cities that Chloe found so beautiful and magical and exotic that she had become quite blasé. However, due in part to her shrewdness and her consideration of Chloe's feelings, she was able to see how much this meant to Chloe and kept her businesslike attitude more subdued than usual. By the noon hour, when Grace brought a cold luncheon into the library for the two women, Chloe had read quite a bit about Mrs. Mainthswaite's business interests in London. Mrs. Mainthswaite had kept a large number of acquaintances as well as business associates from her husband's publishing ventures. She also had some family in England, both in and outside of London itself. It all sounded like a fantasy to Chloe. Travelling to London was like a dream, but to go to Paris as well was beyond her wildest wishes. As well as all of the lovely sightseeing, Chloe would be able to meet many of Mrs. Mainthswaite's business contacts. Perhaps this would prove to be beneficial to her in her writing endeavors.

After partaking of the delicious sandwiches Mrs. Kingston had prepared, Chloe took the tray back to the kitchen, mostly for an excuse of chatting with the cook. She always enjoyed their lunches in the kitchen and jumped at the chance to visit.

"Well, there you are Chloe. We've missed you this week. I hear Mrs. Mainthswaite has been keeping you busy." Mrs. Kingston looked up from the mound of vegetables which she was slicing for dinner.

"Yes she has. I wanted to come say hello though. By the way, how was your weekend Mrs. Kingston? I haven't had the chance to ask you. I hope you enjoyed the pleasant weather."

"Oh my, yes we did. Mr. Kingston and I went to Coney Island. Oh it was marvelous. But a bit crowded and I was glad to be back in my own bed."

"I'm so glad! I have yet to go there myself. Perhaps soon." Chloe sighed and began to place the dishes in the sink, deaf to Mrs. Kingston's protests. She saw how hard the cook worked and it gave her some pleasure to be able to help out when she could. After washing and placing them on the drain board, and listening to an amusing anecdote from Mrs. Kingston, she prepared to go back to work.

"Have a good afternoon Chloe. Oh and you might invite that friend of yours to take you out to Coney Island one day. That would be a pleasant change from the city." Mrs. Kingston's eyes twinkled as she watched the red stain rise in

Chloe's cheeks. She waved Chloe back to work with a laugh and resumed her vegetable chopping.

The rest of the day passed quickly for Chloe, as most days did in the employ of Mrs. Mainthswaite. Chloe once again immersed herself in correspondence from days gone past, which, now put in chronological order, was being outlined for a memoir. Only thoughts of Coney Island and James popped up unbidden like a naughty child who can't sit still. Soon the afternoon was at an end and it was time to think ahead to the evening supper which was always potluck. Chloe walked home, stopping at a delicatessen to purchase some chicken for supper tonight. She changed out of her new suit when she got home, and chose a skirt and one of her new blouses with care. She was pleased with the combination of her slate blue skirt and new ivory cotton blouse. She thoughtfully took along the matching shawl which she had made with the spare material from her skirt. After brushing her hair until it gleamed, pinning it up and grabbing her old hat, she checked her reflection in the pitted mirror in the hall. She went downstairs to meet the other two friends at the park before having their potluck supper. The evening was cooler than the day, although the sun was still high in the sky.

As Chloe waited for her friends, sitting on one of the old stone benches someone had rescued from a fancier locale and had carted to their tiny park, she smiled as she reflected at all of the changes in her life during the time she had lived in the city. She had secured a most promising position with Mrs. Mainthswaite, and managed to enjoy such wonderful times with friends that had come to be as close as family. Even her wardrobe had blossomed, she reflected, as she thought about the meager collection of old fashioned clothes she had brought with her. When she had arrived here she had felt so small and provincial, even her manners were backward in such a cosmopolitan place as this, now she felt at home here, like she could never belong anywhere else, despite her desire for new experiences, this would always remain home. What Chloe did not see was how she had blossomed as well. It showed in her walk and her confidence as she spoke and showed in the new bloom in her cheeks and the way she moved her hands. It was also quite evident that James had noticed this change. As Chloe stood to greet him he glanced appreciatively at her as he took her shawl and hat from the bench without a word and led her over to the low wall which bordered the neighboring churchyard.

"It is such a fine evening isn't it Chloe? I think you and I are under the same impression as to the reason Fiona asked us to meet her here." James spoke softly, aware he should keep the subject matter light, although his eyes remained steady on Chloe's until she flushed and looked downwards to hide her own confused feelings.

"Why, I believe we are." James' perceptiveness surprised Chloe into looking up again to find those brilliant eyes on her. "Oh James, here she comes now!" Chloe was not unaware of the tingle of electricity which passed between the two when James stopped to take her arm as they saw Fiona hurrying toward the park, and she knew before long that the two of them would need to discuss what lay behind that electricity. But this evening was to be about Fiona and by unspoken agreement all other subjects were to be pushed aside.

They met Fiona at the sidewalk, her sparkling eyes matched the tiny gleam on her ring finger and no words needed to be said. Chloe and Fiona ecstatically embraced and started immediately laughing and talking both at the same time while James laughed and interrupted with a cheery, "Come now, I haven't gotten to congratulate Fiona!" He hugged her hard, lifting her off her feet even though she was not much shorter than he.

"Now let's have some dinner before it is too late, shall we?" He took the package which Fiona was carrying and offered an arm to Chloe as they walked back to Chloe's room. They made short work of their potluck supper, which was as delicious as any fancy feast set before a king.

Fiona flopped on the bed, eyes barely straying off of her new ring, smiling to herself as Chloe packed up the rest of the chicken. "Chloe that is one of your new blouses isn't it? It is quite becoming on you. Now we will definitely need to make you a dress so that you can be my bridesmaid."

Chloe smiled; pleased at the compliment as she herself had thought it was a fine outfit. "Oh yes I will need a dress indeed! It's an honor, really Fiona, I am touched."

"Nonsense, you're my best friend. And James, of course you will be there. Oh I know we haven't made any real plans yet, it's to be a long engagement so that we can get the apartment ready, but it's so fun to think about it! We must all get together with Hank soon. I do so want you to get to know him well. And just look at the lovely ring he gave me. Of course I didn't expect this. It's so extravagant, but it was his mother's ring and she wanted him to give it to me." Fiona waved her dainty hand showing off the thin gold circle. "Once we are married I plan to wear it around my neck on a chain." Fiona smiled and blushed. "So when shall we have a get-together?"

"What about Coney Island?" Chloe said without thinking. The others stared her curiously. She blushed. "I thought, I mean, Mrs. Kingston went there this past weekend and made it seem most entertaining. It would be lovely for all four of us to go wouldn't it?" Her eyes fell on James for a second and he smiled in agreement at the fine idea.

The group celebrated jubilantly into the night, At least until Chloe's landlady, passing, gave a vigorous 'hrpmf' to signal her disapproval of a gentleman staying so late. With that, James good naturedly took his leave, closing the door upon the two giggling girls. The girls stayed up into the wee hours, as excitement mounted and choices were weighed, never minding the length of the engagement. Chloe was secretly amused at her friend's unconsciously complacent air of one who is recently betrothed. Already she was becoming the little wife that she had dreamed of in her small attic bedroom. As for Chloe, plans for the upcoming trip and thoughts about James kept her up long after Fiona had left. Finally after what seemed like day's she settled down to sleep for the rest of the night, only to waken at dawn with heavy eyes and aching head.

The day passed mercifully quickly. Chloe did not enjoy it as much as usual, suffering from lack of sleep as she did. She shared her exciting news with Grace and Mrs.

Kingston however, and felt glad from the bottom of her heart whenever she thought about Fiona. Mrs. Mainthswaite chose that day to plan several meetings and was out of the house for several hours. This was just as well, for Chloe was unable to do very much with Mrs. Mainthswaite's correspondence.

She rode the train home as usual, almost falling asleep but for the be-feathered hat on the large woman next to her which kept tickling the back of her neck. The street was busy as usual and Chloe waved a greeting to Mrs. Hall's brother, Bert, he kept telling her to call him on the ground floor of his shop. She went up the stairs and let herself in as her landlady bustled out into the hall.

"Chloe dear, you had a telegram. " She handed Chloe the white slip.

"Me? A telegram?" Chloe frowned, not knowing who would possibly send her a telegram. Only her sister sent letters regularly.

She took the paper and read the few words, which cause her heart to plummet to her feet. It read merely. "Mary sick. Please come home. Father" The telegram fluttered to the ground unheeded as Chloe fought to keep panic from rising.

"What's the matter Chloe?" Mrs. Hall inquired. "Here you better come in and sit down." She shepherded the Chloe through to her private sitting room and sat her down at the table. "I'll make you a cup of tea. You look as though you need it."

67

"No thank you Mrs. Hall. I must start packing. I have to go home." Chloe made to get up when Mrs. Hall arrested her movement.

"Now you stay put. Ten minutes isn't going to make a difference when you need to wait on a train. Sit and tell me what matter is for goodness sake."

"It's my sister. She's sick. It must be bad. The telegram says just to come home." Chloe took the tea, unwanted at first but now the welcome steam revived her. "I have to get a ticket, I have to tell James. And Fiona. And what am I to do about Mrs. Mainthswaite?"

"Alrighty. Let's go about this in an orderly fashion, my dear." Chloe had always found Mrs. Hall's motherly instincts quite comforting but never so much as now. "First I'll send my brother for a ticket. I'm sure the price is about the same. Bert can purchase the next available and get back here by the time you have packed and told your friends. No use worrying about anything when you don't know yet."

Chloe smiled gratefully, swallowed the tea and felt its hot liquid warm her. The late July air was warm in the second floor apartment but Chloe still felt cold and numb with fear. She rose to leave to pack. "Thank you Mrs. Hall, I am in your debt. I don't know how long I'll be gone… I just don't know."

She sat a minute longer blankly staring at the ground "No, no I will go now. I do not know if James is at home of course." Mrs. Hall gave her a pat and told her not to worry about anything and that Bert would be here with the ticket when she returned.

Chloe fairly flew down the few blocks to Fiona's house. Aware that for most families it was the dinner hour, she knocked self-consciously on the door to their apartment. At first glance Fiona saw something was very wrong and led the way up to her attic room, ignoring the concerned glances of her mother.

"What's the matter Chloe?"

Chloe collapsed on Fiona's bed, although every muscle seemed to be taut with nerves. "I got a telegram from home. It said my sister's sick. Mary. I have to go home. " She buried her face in her hands. "Mrs. Hall's brother is getting me a ticket right now."

Fiona knew that a telegram could never mean good news. "It's alright Chloe, of course you have to go back home."

Chloe lifted a pale face "What about James, and Mrs. Mainthswaite? I can hardly walk out on her at this time."

Fiona assured Chloe that she could take care of Mrs. Mainthswaite. However unconventional it may be, Fiona decided to go in person to see Mrs. Mainthswaite tomorrow morning. She then advised Chloe that they should go at once to James' lodging which fortunately would not take long to reach, being only a matter of 9 blocks. Fiona had a talent for taking control in such situations and Chloe, grateful for her friend, followed as meekly as a child.

Quickly Fiona explained the situation to her mother, who agreed with Fiona that she should accompany Chloe, and bade them to be careful. They left through the store, where Fiona's brother, having been given the dinner shift, was helping a harassed young mother balance her basket while keeping her child from rummaging among the dry goods. Before long, they arrived at James' apartment house and found his window lit, fortunately. Fiona stayed in the hall while Chloe went up, knowing instinctively that privacy was required, although Chloe would never have asked.

Chloe knocked timidly on his door and entered when called. James was sitting with his back to her, at a rickety table with a typewriter. Surrounding him were several crumpled papers and a sheaf of notes. His room was small, like hers, but darker. The small bed cowered in a corner under a much worn blanket, and a long table with a hot plate lined the other side of the room. She realized briefly that this was the first time she had been in his room, having only met him on the sidewalk below on occasion. However, she had more important things on her mind at this time. He turned around at the sound of the door swinging inward and gave her a look of amazement and then saw her pale drawn face.

"Chloe, what is it? There is something wrong? Is it Fiona?" James took her by the shoulders and held her at arm's length examining her face critically.

"No she's fine. She is waiting downstairs. It's my sister." Chloe was getting tired of repeating the news, impatient to be on her way, although the interminable train ride would frustrate her even more. "She is sick. I received a telegram this afternoon. I am leaving on the train tomorrow, as soon as my landlady has the ticket. Her brother kindly offered to get it for me." She refrained from explaining that Mrs. Hall gave her brother no choice in the matter.

James let go of her shoulders and took her hands loosely. "I'm so sorry to hear that Chloe. I know you must feel impatient to find out what is happening. I know I would." He gave her hands a gentle squeeze and moved away. Chloe was aware of the loss of warmth as he moved back. "Chloe," James looked at her with an intense emotion in his eyes, "Chloe would you like me to come with you?"

Chloe was startled by his bold suggestion, but gladdened. She felt an almost overwhelming desire to say yes, but at the same time knew that it would be the wrong decision. "I would be very glad of the company indeed, James, but I don't think you should. You have your work here, all this..." she gestured at his stacks by the typewriter. "I don't know how long I will be, and there is no suitable place for you to stay. It's a backwards thinking town." She looked down at her hands, "I do wish you could though." She said softly so he could barely hear her words.

James understood why she had said no, and also how much she appreciated the offer. With this crisis, it seemed as though an understanding, unspoken as it was, had sprung up between them. It was a bittersweet feeling. He noticed now how Chloe was dressed, her thin shirt, suitable for the warm July afternoon but in her stressed state she shivered as though the room was cold. He took a jacket off of his bed and drew it across her shoulders, ushering her downstairs, saying that he would accompany her and Fiona back as it was quite dark now. Fiona was waiting in the hall as promised, and together the three hastened back to Fiona's and to Chloe's and the awaited train ticket.

After leaving Fiona at her door, with promises to inform her of any news, James brought Chloe back to her room where, to her relief, there was a ticket for the train departing at seven-thirty the next morning. James left her in the motherly care of Mrs. Hall after eliciting an agreement to let him accompany her to the train station. With that Chloe returned to her room, refused another cup of tea, Mrs. Hall's cure-all, and promptly went to bed, where sleep eluded her for a long while as her mind whirled with ideas and thought's and fears for her sister.

The next day was a bright morning, the sun seemed to be assuring Chloe that she was doing as much as she possible could, but it was to no avail. Her head ached with lack of sleep. James arrived and the two were soon dispatched in a rattling cab with Chloe's small bag. They did not speak on the way to the station, and James wisely made no move to say comforting and meaningless things to Chloe, knowing it would make no difference. In what seemed like a very short time they were at the station, thanks to the cab. The train was waiting, but it was still early and James followed Chloe onto the train to help her find a seat as she did not waste extra money on first class this time. He stowed her bag for her and stood back to let her pass through.

"Thank you James, for everything. Oh it seems as if I can't find head or tail of myself right now. I just wish that I had more information about my sister." Chloe smiled ruefully, thinking of the long journey ahead.

"Please write anything you can Chloe." James looked down at her tenderly, but Chloe found it easier to avoid his gaze right now.

She nodded looking at the ground. "I'll write to you and Fiona both and let you know what the matter is." More passengers started boarding, jostling past the two.

James made as if to take her hand but thought better of it. "I will be thinking of you then, good bye Chloe. Safe journey." He gave her a brief hard hug.

Chloe was startled by the sudden warmth of James' arms, but it was gone before she could react. She squared her shoulders. "Thank you James for everything, I will write as soon as I can and will see you soon." With a last small smile that softened her formal farewell, she turned away and settled herself in her seat, looking out of the window when and waving when she saw him appear on the platform. She wished she could lean on him right now, and wished more than anything to have his company on the long journey. She needed to be strong though, for she knew not what was waiting for her when she returned to her father's house.

The ride was, as anticipated, long. This time Chloe was not fascinated by the scenes rolling by her window. She remained in her seat when the train made its stops, and leaned back with her eyes closed against the chatter and noise of the third class compartment. She had no desire to speak with anyone. To explain the terrible reason why she should be making the journey. Finally she began to see familiar landscapes and knew within a few hours the train soon would be arriving in Stuflen.

Chapter 10

The station looked the same as it had on that winter day over a year and a half ago. The air was warmer, true, but the town had the same dry frozen atmosphere. No one was waiting for her when she gathered her small bag and stepped off the platform because she had not bothered to send a return telegram. She began the short walk to her house along the familiar streets with a heavy heart. Not many people were out and about, and although she saw some familiar faces, she didn't bother to stop but hurried by. Home. It was home, even though New York City fit her as closely as a second skin. It looked the same, but then she hardly expected it to change as she had changed. The broad porch where she used to sit for hours with her journals was the same, neatly swept but neglected and lonely looking. Quickly she mounted the steps and hesitated on the door step. Should she knock? She didn't feel as if she should walk in unannounced. She settled for a quick knock and then tried the door, which creaked softly as she opened it, looking into the darkened hall. It was quiet, the parlor off to the right had an unused look, and the sun glistened on the crystal vase showing streaks of dust. It was as if the house was holding its breath, like Chloe, against some impending event.

Footsteps sounded on the stairs and she found herself engulfed in a giant hug from her brother Matthew. "Chloe! I am so glad you came. We were not sure if you had received the telegram. Mary gave us your address. I..."

"How is she?" Interrupted Chloe breathlessly, "How is Mary? What's happened?"

"She's got consumption Chloe. Tuberculosis. She's holding her own though, but has lost so much weight naturally. She, she doesn't look as she did when you left, Chloe." Matthew's face was somber but then he smiled, almost forcefully under his strained eyes. "She will be so pleased that you have come. So am I."

Chloe felt the impact of the news hit her like a lightning bolt. Consumption. The very name had a deathly ring to it. How could this happen? Mary had always been so healthy, like a young colt, high in energy and impish laughter. This time Chloe did allow her resolve to weaken and she leaned against her brother for a moment, letting him take her upstairs to the small room which she used to share with Mary. The door was ajar and a light filtered from it.

Mathew turned to her. "Dad is working today. We all take turns at the bank, not wanting to leave her alone for too long, even though we have had help from the neighborhood."

"Is Freddy working too?" Chloe whispered back. The childhood nickname brought a smile to Matthew's lips.

"He is, yes. But they will be back soon. Here, I think Mary is sleeping but let's go in, she will not want to miss you being here."

"I'm hardly leaving, Matthew. Chloe whispered to his back but she wasn't sure if he had heard her. She followed him into the bright room. It had always been very different from the rest of the house in color and décor. The walls were still pale yellow, and there were numerous bouquets of flowers from well-wishers. The curtains were new; a gaily patterned material of bright blue, Mary's favorite color, now graced the large window which looked out at the street below. Mary lay peacefully, her breathing shallow. She made a small mound under the warm coverlet, her slender hands now even thinner lay folded under her cheek. Her face was pale and thin. Matthew made a small noise and Mary opened her eyes and gasped with joy at her sister's face bending over her.

She half rose up beaming at the sight of Chloe but sank back on her pillows coughing. Chloe went to the bed and sat on the edge holding Mary's thin hands in her own.

"Chloe, you came back? I am so happy to see you! But what is the matter? Why are you here? I'm sorry I'm in bed, I have this nagging cough, can't seem to get better very quickly."

Chloe had to physically restrain herself from showing her dismay at how much Mary had changed. Her cheeks had sunken with the weight loss and her eyes overly bright. She seemed unduly pale and weak. "Mary, I came for a visit, is there anything wrong with visiting my favorite sister?"

"Only sister." Mary laughed, causing her to cough a bit and shiver. "My, it's chilly in here, Matthew do you have that window open again?"

"The doctor says to keep the windows open, it's good for you to have the fresh air." Matthew was very serious and his dark eyes reminded Chloe of their father.

"When you get a bit of rest, we can speak more." Chloe chimed in. "Why don't you close your eyes and I will wait for Father downstairs. I will come up in a bit."

"Yes alright," said Mary happily. "Perhaps we can have dinner together. I'm so glad you are here, Chloe." Chloe grasped the thin hands in her own as Mary closed her eyes and settled down in her bed again. With closed eyelids, she resembled the child she had been so much that Chloe fought to keep the tears out of her eyes as she followed her brother down the stairs into the silent kitchen in the back. Chloe found some coffee and made enough for her and Matthew before joining him at the table. Like the rest of the house, the kitchen seemed to be exactly the same as when she left. She supposed vaguely that nothing ever really had changed here while she was growing up. Helping herself to several teaspoons of sugar, she settled back in her chair and looked up at her brother waiting for him to catch her up.

"I suppose she got sick about a month ago that we noticed. It was just a cough and fever at first that wouldn't go away. She had been getting steadily weaker, and has lost so much weight. We considered sending her to a special hospital, but she has been holding her own now and although weak she has not worsened and we don't want to risk the strain of travelling. The doctor is very adamant about her getting fresh air and a good diet, although I cannot say she has improved in her eating habits much." He looked down, slowly stirring his own coffee. "It could go either way at this point, there is not much to do except to keep her spirits up and make sure she has plenty of rest."

"Hmm." Chloe couldn't think of much else to say. She looked out the back window, from which she could see that early evening was beginning to shoot pink and purple streaks across the sky. Soon the temperature would fall. The country didn't hold the heat of the day as much as the city did with its brick and stone. She was devastated at the change in her sister, her face so thin and weak.

"How long are you staying?" Matthew asked. Chloe had kept close correspondence with her sister, and through Mary kept the family informed of her life in New York. She had been filled with joy to find that her other brother Fred had become engaged.

"I don't know." Chloe said quietly. Not even two days ago was she carefree and purposeful in her life with Mrs. Mainthswaite, James and Fiona. James, she thought about him briefly, closing her eyes to see his face. Now she didn't know how long she would be gone, or what was going on. Right now the most important thing was for her sister to get better. Mary had to get better. She sipped at her coffee, chatting with her brother as they waited for the rest of the family to come home. He filled her in on the various happenings in town since she had left, and she recounted several humorous events which had occurred in New York, and described the many different people she had met. It pleased her that she could bring a smile to his face, looking altogether too serious in the wake of her sister's illness. After conferring with her brother and finding that they had a woman in to cook and clean in the mornings, Chloe set about to put the dinner that had been prepared in the oven. They sat for some time, either in comfortable silence or idle chatting, the kitchen dimmed as dusk made its presence known. Chloe tiptoed upstairs several times to peep in at her sister sleeping peacefully. Finally Chloe heard the front door open and close, and went out to greet her father as her brother hastened to light a few lamps.

"Hello Father." Chloe hesitated to display too much emotion in front of him as He had never been that sort of man. She waited in the doorway of the parlor where Matthew had deposited her bag.

"Chloe!" He stopped in the doorway, her brother Fred right behind him. "Come, let me look at you." He stood her at an arm's length and scrutinized her carefully before pulling her in for a brief hug. "You've lost weight."

Chloe realized this was her father's way of implying that she would be better looked after at home, but the hug offset his attitude and she understood his concerns for her welfare were his way of showing affection. Her brother Frederick however was far more demonstrative and fairly lifted Chloe off her feet in a huge bear hug, swinging her around in a circle before setting her down laughing in that hearty booming laugh he always had.

"Mary has been sleeping peacefully for some time." Chloe was glad to report, correctly interpreting her father's involuntary glance at the stairs. It felt good to see her family again, yet so sudden, and unplanned. She had not been prepared for how much of her old feelings flooded back to her and it almost felt as if she had not been gone. Almost, but thoughts of New York; thoughts of all of her friends flitted through her mind and she knew how much she had changed then. She took her brother's arm and led him into the warm kitchen, now filled with a tantalizing smell, while her father went to check on Mary.

"Mary will come down for supper. She generally does if she is feeling well enough. The last few days have been a bit better, but before that she had been growing steadily weaker. We are hoping that the quiet and peace will help her improve quickly. For several weeks she insisted nothing was wrong, you know how Mary can be, and then she wore herself out trying to keep up with everything while she was sick. Once the doctor came in, he made sure she rested and slept. Chloe, I'm so glad you are here, I knew you would come." Fred smiled and took her hand across the table. As always his engulfed her small hand. She smiled back and started grilling him in a playful way about his upcoming nuptials. They spoke of the exciting event which would take place in a few months' time, before the bad winter snows. Presently Mary came down leaning heavily on her father's arm and although weak and wan, was cheerful and carefree. Her infectious laugh kept spirits high, and the family stayed gathered around the large old kitchen table for a long time, talking and laughing, until it was evident that Mary was quite tired.   After Mary retired for the night, accompanied by Chloe who stayed with her until she fell asleep, Chloe joined the rest of the family in the parlor and discussed Mary's condition. It was the firm belief that she was improving, although to Chloe, who had not seen her since she left over a year and a half ago, Mary looked far from healthy. Chloe's father, always a quiet man, stubborn in his own way, sat in his chair brooding, until he demanded to know if Chloe was back home for good.

Chloe was taken aback by the suddenness of his request. "I…No father, I plan to return to New York. I have a life there, a job, friends… Of course it's important that Mary should recover first."

At this her father looked angry and stood, muttering that it was time everyone retired for the night. Chloe dearly would have liked to visit with her brothers, who, as she found, were not so much like her father as she had always assumed. However, her father, still looking slightly perturbed by her firm response, set to putting out lamps and ushering the family upstairs. Apparently he had not changed in her absence.

At the doorway to the spare room, where Chloe would stay, Fred leaned over and whispered, "Don't worry about Dad, Chloe, he will soon realize you have your own life. He sees you as his little girl still."

"I hope so." Chloe murmured back, and gave him a smile as she gently closed the door. She took a deep breath and looked around at the tidy room. It had never been used much. The boys had shared a room always. Once in a while when Chloe was a little girl, her grandparent's had visited, but for the most part, it was used as storage. Clearly it had been dusted and freshened up recently, and Chloe suspected the woman who helped with the cleaning had been keeping it this way. The old wooden headboard and scratched dresser were as she remembered, the braided rug on the floor the same too. Finally there was a chance for her to reflect on the eventful day. She scrambled into her nightgown quickly, pulling her small bag off of the bed where Matthew had deposited it and curled up under the cotton quilt with her newest journal and some loose paper for writing letters. Writing would help her to marshal her thoughts, which right now seemed to be running loose in her head. Naturally her first thought was to write a letter to James, and pulling a sheet of paper toward her, she began to pull together her words. The moon shone through the window beside the bed, sharp and bright in the summer night. Chloe write for a long time, first to James and then a shorter letter to Fiona. Then finally in her journal, some of her most private thoughts and fears, and hopes, and when her eyelids grew heavy and her hand tired from writing, she thrust her pages on the dresser top and fell into a deep and dreamless sleep.

The next morning she awoke to voices. At first she didn't know where she was, the room looked unfamiliar, but the memories flooded back from last night, filling her with worries again. She lay against the pillows looking out into the grassy field beyond the house for a moment before getting up.

The voices grew louder and she realized as she heard her name that her father and one of her brothers must be arguing about her. From the sound, it was Fred. He had always been apt to stick up for her when she was growing up. For the most part the words were inaudible; however she gathered from the tone that father was not pleased that she had not turned up with all of her belongings. She could well imagine that to be the case. After all, he maintained even as the train pulled out of the station when she left, that she would be back after she had realized the city was too big. This thought made her laugh as she pulled on the extra skirt and blouse she had brought. That the city was too big for her was a gross misstatement. She had proven to herself that she could find her way in such a city, and apparently Fred also seemed satisfied. Her father would take a lot longer to accept her as she was however. She heard the front door close loudly and assumed that her father had left for work. Not wanting the confrontation, she had remained in her room until he left, but now descended downstairs to see what she could help with. She found her sister, well wrapped, sitting in an easy chair by the stove. Her cheery smile belied her pale face and gaunt shape, but the persistent cough and weakness showed that her condition was still quite serious.

"Good Morning Mary!" Chloe called, putting a bright expression on her face.

"Chloe, come have some breakfast. Father and Matthew have left for the day. Fred is still here though. There is some fresh bread on the table. Here I'll get some coffee for you." Mary made as if to get up but her movement was arrested by Chloe who insisted on her sitting and resting.

The sisters sat while Chloe munched on the delicious homemade bread and jam. Presently Fred peered in the doorway to tell the sisters he was leaving. He looked at Chloe and grimaced, saying "I expect you heard our argument this morning."

"Yes, what was it about, if I may ask?"

"Mostly you. He doesn't think you will be returning to New York City. He doesn't think you should either for that matter. Naturally he also brought my pending marriage into it as well."

"Why?" Chloe exclaimed "What does that have to do with me or New York?"

"He feels that I am rushing it. I merely said it would be nice to move it up so that you would be able to attend. I would love to have my two favorite sisters there." He grinned.

"Only sisters, you mean." Mary said laughingly. "Off you get now; we shall be just fine here today. Chloe and I have a lot to catch up on."

Fred laughed and nodded, closing the door behind him.

The girls drew sighs of contentment at the quiet, and Chloe decided to follow the doctor's orders and suggested they sit for a while in the sun. The day was quite warm; the last of the July sun was beating down on the roof of the porch and made for a cozy retreat. She settled the two of them, making sure Mary was well wrapped and comfortable. Chloe and Mary sat for several hours in the warm drowsy morning, catching each other up on the events of their lives since they had last corresponded. Mary told Chloe that she had decided to go to college to become a school teacher, a decision she had been pondering, as Chloe had known in letters exchanged. She said when she was well enough father had agreed that she may attend the college nearby.

"It took a lot of pleading I can tell you that." Mary laughed.

Chloe in turn unburdened herself as to her feelings for James and how they had been deepening. She filled Mary in on Mrs. Mainthswaite and Grace and even Mrs. Kingston. She held off on only the trip to Europe. She knew that would be a matter of contention between her and father and since it was apparent that he already disapproved of her life, she didn't want to add more fuel to the fire. Mary listened carefully, occasionally coughing, and sipping at her glass of lemonade. She advised Chloe to listen to her heart, but to always keep her independence, in a manner that was much older than her eighteen years. When Mary seemed to tire, Chloe helped her to her room, making the bed smoothly and plumping her pillows so that it was nice and fresh, and while Mary slept, Chloe made herself useful by giving the house a good sound cleaning. She knew that Elsa Newman's daughter was coming in three mornings a week to cook and clean, but the house was in need of more. Then after checking on Mary several times, she decided to take a short trip to the market and prepare a nice dinner for the family.

Chloe busied herself in the kitchen after coming back from the market, her sister joining her and keeping Chloe company as she moved around the familiar room, the feeling that she had never left as strong as ever. As the afternoon again came to a close for a second day in Stuflen, the rest of the family came home, each assuming roles which they had played before Chloe left. It was, Chloe reflected, so easy to fall into old habits. The evening and night passed pleasantly, although Chloe found that it was best if she avoided her father for the time being and he evidently felt the same as he retired quite early to his room without saying much. That night, again, in the light of the stars and moon, Chloe recorded her thoughts and feelings in her journal, thought with longing of New York, and thought of what may lay ahead, then with no trouble at all she sank into a sleep and dreamt of trains and busy sidewalks with different members of her family popping in and out of the dream. The next day she awoke refreshed and well before anyone else in the household. Savoring the quiet of dawn and wandering downstairs to gaze at her familiar yet new surroundings, she wondered again what lay before her. Her desire to return was strong, yet she could see, more than perhaps the other members of her family that her sister was not going to make a full recovery, no matter how optimistic the doctor had been. She heard her cough and watched her struggle to breathe when involved in the least strenuous of tasks, and she knew deep down that her sister was not going to be able to lead the independent life that she longed for. Chloe felt bitterness at this thought. Why was it that Chloe was able to make her way, make a life, however hard it had been to begin, when Mary had little hope of that? This filled her with a sadness which lasted through the day. It seemed the weather matched her mood, as clouds began to fill the sky in late afternoon, darkening prematurely and driving the children who played at the end of the street to seek the refuge of their houses earlier than usual. Not surprisingly the rain began overnight and stayed, stagnant over the little town for several days. During this time Chloe managed the house and planned meals and her family quickly grew used to having her there.

The steady rain kept Chloe from visiting the post office where she had hoped to mail another letter to Fiona. She had not written one to James aside from the first, since she didn't know what to write. Her resolve was as strong as ever to regain her life in the city, yet familial obligations and the continued realization that her sister would remain weak, had made her question her choices. It seemed that Matthew had fallen in with her father's wishes and assumed she was staying, yet her sister and Fred were still cheerfully speaking of visiting her in the city in a year's time. In what seemed like a blur of days so similar to each other, a week had passed since Chloe had made her impulsive flight west to her sister's bedside. Mary had not felt well over the weekend, and stayed in bed with Chloe hovering at her side. It seemed she had overdone herself and the cough had worsened. This further strengthened the weighty fear that Chloe had and she grew more apprehensive about leaving her sister. That Sunday Chloe decided to write to James again, this time laying out all of her fears and doubts. She attempted to put as much of herself in the letter, and her feelings, since she knew how well he returned those, but also her familial obligations. How strong would those be, and how much would Mary need her strength in the future?

Chapter 11

That Wednesday, the weather was warm and sunny again and Mary came outside with the help of Chloe to rest on the porch.

"But you must go back to New York!" Mary exclaimed at Chloe's noncommittal response regarding her plans. "It's where you are meant to be. I can feel that as well as you." She looked severely at Chloe, giving such a schoolmarm's look that Chloe had to laugh and then soberly remembered that Mary probably would not be able to fulfill that dream.

"I don't know Mary. It's not that I don't want to… but I can write well enough here." Chloe reached out to brush a strand of Mary's dark locks out of her face and continued. "I worry about you Mary, you can't manage the house by yourself, and Father is being so obstinate."

"I know. " Mary sighed. "He and Matthew are, I feel, not supportive of your dreams at all. You have always been ambitious and yet they never understood that. They still feel that we women should be in the kitchen." She laughed bitterly, which set of a spasm of coughs. Chloe handed her a glass of water and waited until Mary drank and then wearily leaned back on the cushions that Chloe had piled around her.

"They do have such an old fashioned view. And what about you Mary, how are you, really and honestly?"

Mary looked down at her thin hands, tracing the pattern on the light crocheted blanket on her lap. "Some days are better. Chloe, I know that I will not be able to teach. I don't feel bad about it; my life is going to take another path. Father has not realized that I am not going to recover completely, but I can feel it. I think that in time I will be able to tutor students from home and of course I'll always have my poetry."

Chloe knew that Mary had always been able to put words together in ways that Chloe with all of her talents in prose could never do. Mary always had one foot in fairyland. That's what their brother Fred said. "I'll always have a home here and who knows what will happen in the future. We are both so young. Which is why you need to go back to New York City. I dearly love having my only sister here but I don't want you wasting your life on my account."

Chloe, not completely reassured despite her sister's bright words said nothing at this. She thought she would wait and see. She hoped to see a letter from Fiona or perhaps James soon. The days tumbled together, Mary's cough and weakness, although not as much of an acute worry was lingering and the doctor was unsure as to if her lungs would recover properly from the tuberculosis. Finally one bright afternoon a full two weeks from when Chloe first found the telegram, Chloe was making her daily haunt of the tiny post office tucked in a corner of the general store when she was rewarded by a letter from both Fiona, and, unexpectedly, Mrs. Mainthswaite. Eagerly she tore them open and scanned first Fiona's and then Mrs. Mainthswaite's. Mrs. Mainthswaite's was written on heavy ivory stationary, expensively and elegantly penned. She inquired after Chloe's sister, having heard from Fiona, and reassured Chloe that her post was available to her when she felt it was the right time to return. She begged Chloe to please not rush and wished her well. The reassurance and care that showed in Mrs. Mainthswaite letter brought tears to Chloe's eyes and her indecision about her future strengthened. She resolved to write back to Mrs. Mainthswaite that very night. Putting this aside, she quickly walked back home as fast as seemly to read Fiona's letter in the privacy of her room. A sharp pang stabbed at her when she saw that there had been no letter from James, but perhaps Fiona had some news, or perhaps he had not had time to write back. Once reaching the house and unburdening herself of her various groceries, she looked in on her sister who was busy at her desk, spectacles charmingly askew on her thin face. Once in her room she let her guard down and scrutinized Fiona's thick missive with her heart beating hard in anticipation of at the very least some news from James or of James.

Fiona's letter was almost like speaking with her in person. It was in her chatty breezy style, full of news of her daily life and of Hank and her engagement. She wrote how hopeful she was that Chloe's sister was recovering, and that she hoped to meet her one day. Her mentions of James were not as numerous as Chloe had hoped. Fiona mentioned how hard James had been working but that he had stopped by the store once or twice. Apparently he had not done much else but to tell Fiona he too had gotten a letter from Chloe. Reading and rereading this, Chloe had to swallow hard to contain her disappointment. She wondered why James did not write, was he indeed as busy with work as he had indicated to Fiona, or was it something else, something she had written perhaps? Had her doubts about her sister's health put him off? Chloe shook herself at the thought. It would not do any good to brood. If James was too busy to bother replying she would not concern herself with it. She had too many other worries and decisions on her mind. But there was a small part of her which still wondered and was hurt by his silence.

Chloe looked up at her door opening and was relieved to find Mary standing in the hall with a puzzled look upon her face.

"What's wrong Chloe?"

"Nothing, I was just reading a letter from Fiona."

Mary understood at once. "No letter from James? What did Fiona say? Any news?"

"No."

"Well there are many reasons, as you know the mail could have been delayed, or most probably he has been quite busy." Mary knew that James and Chloe had a complicated friendship, which shouldn't be as complicated as it was. Sometimes after reading Chloe's letters she felt quite exasperated with her older sister's unwillingness to see what was right in front of her. "At any rate you will be going back to New York soon and I am sure it will be a happy reunion."

"Yes..." Chloe, still undecided about many things was unable to reply with conviction. In her heart she knew she would not be happy here, but what did that matter when it came to her sister's health.

"You will be going back Chloe." Mary said sharply, causing Chloe to glance up in surprise at her tone. "Please stop thinking nonsense about staying here Chloe. I have no delusions that I am going to recover fully. I know I will be weak and that my lungs will be bad for the rest of my life, but I am fine. You have your life to live, so go live it."

"But...Mary...I."

"No Chloe, I know father thinks I will be married off in no time with a family soon after, I know he thinks that you will stay, but do not give him that satisfaction. You made a stand when you left a year and a half ago and you cannot back track! My life has changed but I am HAPPY. You are not, dear sister." Mary gave her a stern look to emphasize her speech, managed not to cough and turned squarely on her heel and marched downstairs again.

Chloe sat on her bed, stunned by the firm determination behind Mary's speech. Half angry at Mary and half proud of her sister, she considered what Mary said. It was all truth. She was the one mooning about with indecision while Mary was determined to make her life as best she could with her new limitations. Perhaps she was right, after all, Chloe belonged in New York and had friends and a job there. A small voice in her head asked, "What of James?" but an even larger voice said it didn't matter, her career was there, her life was there. She sat that way, gazing unseeingly out of the window, for a long time. Finally the August dusk began to fall, and she heard the door and voices downstairs which brought her out of her reverie. She shook herself and went downstairs to join the family and to tell her father that she was, again, leaving his house.

Chapter 12

The evening did not go well. Chloe made her quiet announcement as she served dinner, and although Mary and Fred looked at her proudly, she had sat in silence for a good half hour listening to both her father and brother Matthew berate her for leaving while Mary had yet recovered. Mary valiantly stuck up for her sister, and Chloe disputed false claims such as the real reason behind her leaving was a man. After failing to receive a letter from James, Chloe had felt a sadness and insecurity, but her sister's strong words had reminded her of her driving ambition and the reason why she had made such a journey in the first place. Finally after Chloe's father ran out of reasonable arguments, the rest of the dinner was eaten in silence. One by one her father and brothers retreated to the parlor while Chloe and Mary washed up, then proceeded to retire to Mary's room. Presently Fred knocked softly on the door and looked in on Chloe lying limply on Mary's bed while Mary busied herself with embroidery, her thin fingers working elegantly.

"When do you plan on leaving Chloe?" Fred asked as he sat on the edge of the desk which had been Chloe's so long ago.

"I don't know Fred. I suppose soon. I cannot bear much more of father's anger. I will miss your wedding." Chloe looked sorrowfully at her brother.

"That's alright Chloe, we had decided that we should wait until Mary was stronger anyway, Mary is to be the maid of honor. By springtime the flowers will be in bloom and that is fine with Gertie. She had wanted an outside wedding anyway. You will be able to come after all. But even if you weren't, I... we would understand." He glanced at Mary and took Chloe's hand gently. "Chloe, we know how much you need to be back in New York. This place is suffocating you. It always has, although I was too stubborn to see that before, I see it now."

"Well, I still feel that I should stay a bit longer, perhaps Mary..." Chloe trailed off as her received an indignant prod from her sister.

"Don't use my health as an excuse. I am perfectly well, if not a bit weak. You have been away two weeks, and should not be gone three."

"Perhaps by the end of the week then. I will make some arrangements to have Elsa's daughter start coming in to help with the house. You are not to be overexerting yourself."

"Don't worry about that Chloe," Fred laughed, "I will make sure she keeps quiet." He stood, stretching, "I will miss your cooking Chloe to be sure." He tipped a wink at the sisters and left the room closing the door quietly.

Chloe looked at Mary. "Well, I suppose it would do no good to write back to Fiona if I am to be back in New York next week. I will miss you."

"And I you." But, Mary put aside her needlework. "It's time we get some sleep, and tomorrow will be another day."

The next few days were a whirlwind of activity, unusual for Chloe to experience in the confines of her hometown. Her sister, feeling strong enough to venture out, accompanied her sister to call upon an old friend of Chloe's for luncheon. It was a lovely afternoon, mild enough still to sit outside on the tiny patio which ran along the back of her friend's house. Chloe received the long awaited letter from James. It filled her with more confusion than it did reassurance, for its style was friendly yet oddly impersonal. He stayed away from any personal subjects and wrote how busy he had been and that he hoped that Mary was making more of a recovery. Chloe sadly folded the letter into the back of her journal, and tried not to make much of its meaning.

She spent quite some time washing the small amount of clothes she had brought and making sure that the house was as spic and span as she could get it. She also visited the market, making sure there was plenty in the pantry and that Dulcie Newman would be back in mornings to assist with the household chores and cooking. In this way Chloe could feel confident that she was leaving her sister in good hands and not in any danger of overexerting herself. Chloe's father, who had blindly assumed Chloe would be staying, finally resigned himself, with much help from Fred, Chloe suspected, to the fact that she was indeed returning to New York, and exhibited less anger than he did on her arrival. The last evening was filled with gaiety and light. Fred had invited his fiancé to dinner, and the family feasted and laughed into the night, only when Mary, yawning uncontrollably rose from her seat by the parlor fire, declare herself on the verge of sleep did the party realize how late it had gotten. Chloe enjoyed the night immensely and found quite a sympathetic soul in Fred's fiancé. After many good nights and promises to return for the wedding, Fred had seen his fiancé home with a glow of satisfaction. Chloe soon followed her sister and was fast asleep in a matter of seconds. She had barely any time to reflect on the subject of James, as she was wont to do before turning in each night. Before very long, she would be back in her rusted wrought iron bed in New York, and the necessity of letters would no longer be important.

Chapter 13

The next day dawned gray and sullen and a heavy rain prevented Mary from accompanying the family to the train station. Chloe said goodbye to her father and brother Matthew that morning, since he felt it was better that they be at the bank. Her father returned her stiff hug with his own and a cold peck on the cheek which was as affectionate as she had seen him. Mathew, always her father's son, did not say much as he shared Father's opinion that Chloe should stay and keep house. He did however give her a warm hug and promised that he would visit in time. They departed on good terms. Being the son of the bank manager did have its benefits, and Fred elected to accompany Chloe to the train at noontime. The two sisters sat in the warm kitchen sharing a last heart to heart, for a while at least.

"Now make sure to write as often as possible Chloe. I promise I'll respond. And do not worry about James. I'm sure it will work out to the best."

"Yes I will write often. We shall see what happens on my arrival. At least this time I have a place to live and a wonderful job." Chloe smiled happily, but her heart was heavy at the thought of missing her sister. She knew she would miss her even more than before, especially since Mary was unable to be as independent as she had hoped.

Some of these thoughts must have shown on Chloe's face, for Mary smiled back and said, "Don't worry so much, I may not have the strength I once had, but my ambition and passion has not lessened. Next time you come back I expect you will find things have changed." She patted Chloe's hand and looked at the clock. "You had better get going. You don't want to miss your train.

Chloe felt as if her sister had taken on the role of oldest, and was proud yet saddened at this new maturity. She wished it could be she that was comforting Mary, yet it seemed the other way around. Off Chloe went, with her brother Fred who waited patiently in the small waiting area of the tiny train station. The cold rain dripped down unceasingly. Its staccato was at last drowned by the sound of the train pulling into the station. Chloe hefted her bag and turned to get on the train. She looked back at her brother, who, shielding his head from the rain came to hug her one last time.

"Oh Fred. I wish I knew if this was the right thing to do. I don't know, I mean I am worried about Mary."

"Mary is stronger than any of us put together I believe. You know she will be fine. We will all be fine and in time Dad will come around. He needs to believe you are happy in New York. You know he has his ideas. Now, in you go before we both get drenched." With that he playfully pushed her into the train and stood back under the overhang.

The last Chloe saw of him was his grin under his dripping hat. She settled herself back in her seat and watched the fields roll past the window with a satisfaction and sadness as well. It was a much different feeling than the last time she had ridden towards the East. No fear of the unknown gripped her with exhilaration as before. This time, her excitement was for people and things that she knew. However she did experience a certain amount of trepidation about her arrival. Why had James not written more than in his letter and what was he doing? She spent some time pondering these questions. At any rate she would soon know once she got back home, and spoke with Fiona. Home, she was already calling New York home again, like she had for the past year and a half. While visiting her family she had quickly slipped into her old attitude and was disturbed by how easily Stuflen had become 'home' again. She spent some time staring out of the windows, dripping with rain, contemplating different reasons why James would not have written until she realized with a start how she was turning the same thought over and over and was becoming quite tiresome to herself. Shaking herself vigorously to dispel the negative thoughts, much to the amusement of a young boy in the next row, she closed her eyes and attempted to doze. The rocking of the train proved most effective and the next time Chloe opened her eyes it was dark. Realizing she had not eaten much, she opened the small picnic lunch her sister had thoughtfully made her for the journey and ate hungrily. Most of the people in the train, not very full, were asleep. Most were like her, small bags, hampers of food, most likely visiting family. Feeling quite full after a delicious cold supper, she settled back in her seat again and prepared to doze for as much of the remaining journey as she could.

Bright lights streamed in the window, momentarily blinding a very groggy Chloe, and then cooler darkness prevailed as the train entered the station. Her excitement abounded as she realized they had almost reached their destination, and she eagerly looked around at the familiar sights. Gathering her belongings together and swiftly exiting the train when it finally came to a stop, she hurried through the station and into the street, breathing a deep breath of satisfaction as the city welcomed her with open arms.

Chapter 14

"Chloe, I truly haven't seen much of James in the three weeks you have been gone. He stopped by twice the first week and then once last week to see whether I had any news from you. He mentioned that he had written once and also has been working quite a lot on several projects and declared his intention of becoming quite the sought after reporter. He looked tired, to be completely honest. You need to take some time, you've only just arrived back home. And no worrying about James. Chloe, the man has been patient with you; we both know how he feels. "

"Do we?" Said Chloe quickly.

Fiona looked at her dear friend with a certain amount of exasperation and of superiority, the superiority of being comfortable with her own Hank. "Yes we do know, Chloe, I have seen the way he looks at you, and I have seen that for quite a long time while you have been confused about your feelings for him. It's perfectly natural, of course." Fiona hastened to add, seeing her friend's hurt expression. "But you must know that no one has infinite patience, not even James. I do believe that he has decided to concentrate on his career right now. I'm sure he will be thrilled to find you home safe and sound."

Chloe nodded slowly realizing the meaning of her friend's sage words. "I pushed him away in my eagerness to further my own career as a writer, and because I just was so unsure of myself. And my last letter was filled with uncertainty. I'm not unsure now, and here we are. It is ironic that now I must be the one to search him out."

"Are you not unsure anymore Chloe?" Fiona asked with a smile.

"No. Not anymore. But now it might be too late." Chloe flopped back on the bed and sighed. "What am I to do Fiona?"

"We'll send him a telegram. It won't cost so very much. Tell him you are home and are looking forward to seeing him so much. It would be better than walking over; he is surely not at home. He will get it and with luck, come by after you have done your work with Mrs. Mainthswaite. You are going tomorrow Chloe?"

"Yes, I had sent a telegram telling her I was on my way home."

"Ok then it's settled." Fiona sat back with a satisfied air and surveyed Chloe. "We should send him a telegram now." With that she ushered Chloe from her room. That afternoon Chloe walked back to her room alone, after leaving Fiona. She felt much better after speaking with her friend and finally getting off her chest the feelings that had been weighing her down. She felt lighter, yet at the same time unsure of what would happen with James. Had he grown tired of waiting? Fiona's words had opened her eyes and she wondered why it took her so long to recognize what was right in front of her, and why she had been so afraid of it. She wished she had said more when they last saw each other, but her fears about her sister were overshadowing everything. Had he known? She chided herself for questioning how he felt about her when it seemed to be obvious to Fiona. Why had it not been so to her? That was a question she could not answer in full. She spent the rest of the evening unpacking the few things that were left in her small bag, and cleaning the dusty room. Mrs. Hall popped her head in at one point to give Chloe a plate of stew which she declared would only go to waste. Chloe, knowing full well that Mrs. Hall would never throw away this much food, accepted gratefully. She felt lucky to have such a landlady who was such a motherly caring person. After bringing the dish back to Mrs. Hall she went back to her room, brought out her journal and sat in her customary seat by the window, where she could survey the street down below, now darkened but still full of sounds. She spent several long hours lost in thoughts and pages. Exhausted at last, she climbed into bed, pulled the light sheet over her head and promptly fell into a dreamless sleep.

The next morning she presented herself at Mrs. Mainthswaite's house as though the last three weeks had not even happened. Indeed it had however, and Chloe felt as if the sickness and worry and journey had aged her beyond her twenty-three years. Grace and Mrs. Kingston were overjoyed to see her back and even Mrs. Mainthswaite bestowed one of her rare crusty smiles on Chloe as she bent her elegant silver head in the direction of the library and told Chloe that she was very pleased that Chloe was back. Chloe sighed in happiness looking around the light and spare room, once again immersed in this literary world. Not for the first time, Chloe was hit with such a sense of belonging; she realized that there really had never been any other place for her than this beloved city.

The day flashed by. Chloe felt surrounded by the things she loved and immersed herself in her work determined to work harder than ever for Mrs. Mainthswaite and to gain the time she had lost. Soon it was the end of the day and Chloe took her leave, the nervousness and uncertainty about James returning almost as soon as she gained the sidewalk outside of Mrs. Mainthswaite's. She was unsure if he would come after receiving a telegram. She tried to tell herself that everything was fine, but of course she could not know.

Sitting on the rocking train, the noise of it almost drowning out the chatter of other passengers, she decided she would walk by the store to see Fiona, instead of going to the small market two doors down. She could replenish her small pantry, and see Fiona at the same time. Fiona was at the counter helping two elderly ladies with their purchase and waved to Chloe as she walked by on her way to the back. After choosing several items, and some fresh bread made by Fiona's mother that morning, along with some coffee and sugar, she paid for the groceries and chatted with Fiona for a few minutes. Leaving the shop she impulsively bought a small bunch of flowers from a stand on the corner. Spicy smelling chrysanthemums would liven up her room and bring back the lived in feel. Laden with her groceries and flowers she trundled back to her room realizing that perhaps she had been postponing her arrival in hopes that it would bring James. However when she gained the sidewalk across from her bright blue door, there was no sign of him. Sighing disconsolately, she crossed the street and opened the door awkwardly balancing one bag on a hip while tucking the flowers under her arm. In truth James would not be finished with his work day until much later. She resigned herself to a solitary dinner, imagining herself having many more of these when Fiona had married and would no longer be available for carefree jaunts in their tiny pocket park. After dinner, which was actually quite pleasant, she sat on the small stoop outside the blue door and enjoyed some conversation with one or two passersby down below with whom she was acquainted. Chloe went up to Mrs. Hall's apartment, thanking her landlady profusely for all of her help during her absence during Mary's illness. Brushing it aside, Mrs. Hall laughed cheerily and mentioned that she was glad Chloe was back as it had been too quiet. "I miss hearing the chatter when your friends come visiting. How's that young man of yours?"

Chloe smiled noncommittally and murmured something about him being busy before retreating back to the privacy of her room to mull over the reasons for James' silence. She had hoped that upon receiving the telegram from her, a necessity since there was no telephone at either house, he would naturally rush over as soon as he was able. She knew his feelings for her were not imagined, and yet she regretted holding back and pushing his tentative advances away. She had truly not wanted to disturb such a golden friendship and had also been quite disconcerted to find that her feelings for him were more than friendship. Long had she battled for independence in her own life, only to find herself yearning such companionship. Now that she knew her own feelings, it was impossible not to fear that James had changed his, however unlikely that might be in three short weeks. As much as Chloe despised herself for waiting and hoping to see James, she could not help herself. She sat by the window, blankly looking out, enmeshed as she was in her own thoughts, that the distant bong of the clock startled her and she realized how late it had become. Dispiritedly she realized James would not show up at this late hour and she retired to bed. The next day, she woke with a dull pounding headache which matched the sullen drizzle. Quickly she got herself ready for work and prepared to leave, noting with dismay the worn condition of her umbrella. Sighing and snatching her old battered hat and jamming it on her head she headed out the door. As always when faced with the prospect of what the day would hold at Mrs. Mainthswaite's, her spirits lifted and she started planning what she would do for the day. She remembered with a thrill, that the much awaited trip to England was only weeks away, and lost in imagining the trip in detail, and all of the experience she would gain, she hurried through the light rain with her head down. Reaching the train platform she was startled when a figure loomed over her. Looking up she saw to her amazement that James was standing at the top of the stairs with his umbrella grinning at her astonishment.

"James! I hardly expected to see you this morning, and on the train platform, and in the rain!" She couldn't keep the smile off of her face or out of her voice, and finally Chloe had no logical reason to hide her happiness.

He smiled back and ushered her under his umbrella. "I wanted to come last night, but it was late by the time I reached home and received your telegram. I'm afraid I have been working night and day lately But how are you? I am so glad your sister has recovered. Come I'll ride the train with you. I have some business in the area." Together the two boarded the train which had pulled in with its deafening rattles and clanks.

"I am well, thank you James." Chloe felt the stain spread across her cheeks as she brushed his arm and her heart give a thump. "My sister will never be as she was, but we are thankful she is no longer in danger. She is a strong girl and will find ways to regain her independence. I saw Fiona yesterday. She mentioned how busy you have been."

"Yes I have, it's been an amazing few weeks, and I feel that I am really starting to make a name for myself and soon I hope to be considered as a serious journalist." He spoke with passion and Chloe envied him momentarily the opportunities that he had and the happiness that they were bringing him. This only lasted a moment as she thought about her own future; a chance to travel was something they had both dreamed of. Besides she was genuinely glad that he was so happy and ambitious. She glanced into his face, into those brilliant blue eyes which always seemed to look into her core. She listened as he spoke about his ideas and plans, long hours he had been keeping. She in turn told him that the impending trip was still on schedule for England, and he expressed simple happiness at her opportunities. As they talked she felt a sense of sadness, but about what she was not sure.

Presently the train pulled up to her stop and she rose preparing to take her leave of James and make her way to work. She was surprised when he accompanied her on the same route, surprised but pleasantly so. The two walked companionably over the few blocks to the quiet avenue where Mrs. Mainthswaite's lived and there James left her with a tip of his cap.

"I don't want to make plans and break them Chloe, but I would like to get together with you and Fiona this week. I don't know if I will be available tonight. Shall I send word when I find out?" Chloe agreed to this, looking forward to the evening.

James laughed lightly and gave her a nudge on the arm. "That's all wonderful news to hear from you. I'm glad everything is back to normal." Chloe wasn't sure how to react to this slightly enigmatic and disappointing declaration but before she could he was off with a wave of his hat. She walked the rest of the way to Mrs. Mainthswaite's under cover of her patched umbrella; however the drizzle somehow found its way underneath. Gaining the house with its sophisticated air, she entered the quiet and timeless hall, listened to the tick of the clock, and paused to hand her damp outer garments to Grace before passing into the library. Mrs. Mainthswaite was not in the library; most likely she was employed in other tasks this morning, so Chloe sat at her table and got right to work. Trying to shake off the vague feeling of disappointment from her encounter with James, she immersed herself in the past and was startled when the door opened and Mrs. Mainthswaite bustled in. Commending Chloe on the work she had finished, she declared that she needed to do a few errands as well as post some letters to contacts in England, in preparation for their upcoming voyage. Chloe smiled and accepted the compliment from Mrs. Mainthswaite happily, rare as they were, and prepared to get back to work when Grace came in and asked Chloe if she would like to join them for lunch. Surprised that it was lunchtime already, Chloe agreed and followed the diminutive maid back to the kitchen where Mrs. Hall had cooked up a hearty soup and fresh bread. It was a welcome feast for even with the August heat, the rain made it seem damp and chilly.

"I must say Chloe it's been awfully quiet here without you the past few weeks, although I would not say it was ever loud, but you know what I mean." Mrs. Kingston spooned out the rich thick soup into large bowls and cut three chunks of bread before sitting comfortably down at the massive round table with the other two.

"Oh I agree. Chloe it's just so nice to have you back." Little Grace piped up in her lilting tones, reminding Chloe as always of a fairy. Mary would have found her quite enchanting.

"It's good to be back. It was so busy yesterday I hardly saw you. I have looked forward to our lunch time confabs." Chloe smiled at the two and sipped the gently steaming soup. "Mrs. Kingston you have outdone yourself! This soup is delicious!"

"Oh thank you dear. Mr. Kingston is working outside today, and in this damp weather, I thought a nice soup would be just the thing." She paused and asked delicately, "now, I am glad your sister is well again, but do I detect a bit of gloom in your eye?"

Chloe stirred uncomfortable under Mrs. Kingston's unerring instincts. "Yes Mary is doing as well as can be expected. She will never regain as much strength as she had but at least she will be healthy." Chloe had grown weary of repeating the same thing about her sister. "It's just one of those depressing dark days, hard to be cheerful when it is so damp."

"That's true, and how is your friend James?"

"Oh, he is fine, very busy lately. He has been very successful lately but of course that means more work." Chloe avoided anything but the most general since she really had no idea where she stood anymore."

"Really Mrs. Kingston, you needn't pester Chloe with all of these questions." Grace admonished with a laugh. "She has hardly had time to eat her soup for all of our prying."

Chloe laughed. "That's quite all right; it's just nice to have such good friends."

The three chatted on about this and that; Grace filling Chloe in on the happenings in and out of the household until the back door was heard and Mr. Kingston came in, covered with damp and wiping his boots on the stoop. Chloe greeted him with a smile and took the opportunity to retreat back to the library and settle herself back into work until such time as Mrs. Mainthswaite returned.

"Chloe you have made even more progress than I expected." Mrs. Mainthswaite told her as she examined what

Chloe presented. "This looks quite satisfactory. Now, I have procured our tickets and also arranged to have rooms reserved once we arrive in London. We shall sail on the twenty-eighth, in 2 weeks tomorrow. I imagine that this leaves you enough time to complete the rough outline that you are working on. You may go now; I have a dinner to attend and need to prepare for it."

Chapter 15

Chloe bid her employer good bye and ducked into the kitchen once more to wave to Mrs. Kingston who had wrapped up a loaf of her delicious bread for Chloe. Grace was not in evidence, most probably finishing her afternoon duties. In such a small household as this, Grace had less work than some of her contemporaries who were employed by much stricter families.

After stopping by Fiona's and eliciting a promise from Fiona to join her for a cold supper, she stopped at a cart on the street for two sandwiches. On arrival at home, she knocked briefly on her landlady's door and presented her with the bread, wrapped in brown paper. In her own room she lay the two sandwiches on her table and saw an envelope lying on the floor. Evidently someone in the household had pushed it under her door if it had come in the post that morning. It was from James, and said quite simply that he was unable to get away tonight, but that he was eager to stop by the next evening. It was a thoughtful gesture just as meeting her at the station this morning had been. Perhaps Chloe had imagined the ever so slight difference in James demeanor. His friendly but almost chummy air. Perhaps once they spent more time together Chloe could feel more reassured as to how James felt about her. In truth she had not spared many thoughts for him throughout her busy day, so immersed in work had she been, but now, having a few hours before Fiona arrived, she found herself worrying unnecessarily, and chided herself for becoming one of those dreamy girls always mooning about romantic entanglements. "Really Chloe", she told herself, "You are an independent woman and above such nonsense." With an effort she attempted to concentrate on other more pleasant thoughts such as ships and England but thoughts of James kept intruding, until she gave up, flopped back on her bed and stared moodily at the ceiling until Fiona came. After a night of laughter and gossip, Chloe felt much more herself than she had in weeks, and fell into a dreamless sleep only to wake to another cloudy dreary day. This did not dampen Chloe's spirits however. She was looking forward to another productive day in the library, amid the stacks of papers Mrs. Mainthswaite had so carefully kept. She dressed briskly and hurried down the street, not stopping to buy her customary bun since she could have some of Mrs. Kingston's delicious bread when she arrived at her employers. She hesitated briefly at the train stop, looking around for James, but scolded herself for that and firmly pushed him out of her mind for the day.

  That evening James showed up at the duly appointed hour, smiling warmly and invited her to dinner. The two had a lovely time out and although Chloe remained as unsure of him as ever, more so in fact, she was determined not to let that uncertainty show. If James chose friendship with her, then perhaps that was what she truly needed. More time to concentrate on her writing and her employment with Mrs. Mainthswaite. Thus the next few weeks passed in the same manner. Chloe enjoyed her occasional dinners immensely with James, and tried to ignore the sadness which had crept into her thoughts. She and Fiona saw as much of each other as possible, and Fiona's bubbly enthusiasm about Chloe's impending voyage and also her own engagement was quite infectious. The two girls did some minor shopping to prepare for Chloe's trip and poured over endless ideas for Fiona and Hank's simple wedding. At Mrs. Mainthswaite's house, there was also an air of excitement as Grace scrambled to ready her mistresses' trunks for such a long trip. They would be gone for approximately 6 weeks. Finally the day before they were to leave arrived, and instead of working through to her usual early evening time, Chloe was shooed out of the library to take care of any last minute preparations.

"I shall send the carriage" said Mrs. Mainthswaite, who always claimed to keep the horses just for Mr. Kingston's enjoyment. "Be ready at seven o'clock tomorrow morning please, I do not want to get caught up in the usual mob when boarding the ship." Chloe nodded nervously, trying to act as if she too was a seasoned traveler like Mrs. Mainthswaite. The older lady nodded her elegant head and ushered her out into the street, where the oven-like air was scented with the late flowers in the elegant gated garden. Chloe fairly ran down the street, almost colliding with a portly mustached gentleman who frowned at her youthful energy. She skipped up the steps to the train platform and waited impatiently. Finally after what seemed like an age, she was home. That night was to be a special one. The three friends were finally able to gather together, something that had proved exceedingly difficult owing to James' new journalistic endeavors. Chloe checked her trunk for what seemed like the twentieth time that week and stacked a few last minute items which would need to be packed tomorrow morning. After she changed into one of her more stylish outfits and studied her hair in the mirror before finding it satisfactory, she sat down to await her company. Fiona arrived first with her newly betrothed in tow, carrying a heavy basket smelling suspiciously like her mother's cooking. As they waited they engaged in desultory conversation which Chloe found hard to concentrate on, as excited as she was about the morrow. Hank was a pleasant young man, much quieter than Fiona, but Chloe surmised that would work to the couple's advantage. He proved a good addition to the little group. Not long after, James's footstep was heard on the stairwell, and the group went to join him, having been given the use of Mrs. Hall's dining table for the occasion as she was spending the evening with her brother's family. The group celebrated long after the delicious stew was gone, and as they munched on delicacies from the Italian bakery that James always frequented, Chloe reflected that for the first time since she had been back, she caught a faint glimmer of the tenderness that she had grown used to when she looked at James. Although she had tried hard to ignore the pangs of sadness which engulfed her from time to time during the past few weeks, she felt overjoyed to see his eyes so intent upon her face. She could feel the blush under his glance, and avoided Fiona's keen eyes with an effort.

"How do you stay so calm Chloe? Really if I was about to embark on such a trip, I should be utterly beside myself with excitement, but also scared." Fiona glanced affectionately at Hank, murmuring in an undertone that she could never bear to be away from him anyway. Chloe caught the obvious affection between the two and suddenly felt lonely and clumsily tried to cover her feelings with a few jokes and light banter. Finally Fiona stood, announcing that they should go as it was to be an early morning for Chloe.

"Before I leave, I have something for you." Fiona told her with a mischievous twinkle in her eye.

"What is it?" Chloe exclaimed "I have everything I need for the trip. She looked at James questioningly.

"Don't look at me." He protested, bright eyes flashing at Chloe warmly. Hank grinned at them amiably, ruffling his brown hair as he waited for Fiona.

Fiona rustled in her basket for a moment before straightening up and holding out something pink and silky in her hands.

"Why, why it's a dress Fiona! It's beautiful! But however…?"

"I borrowed a skirt and shirt when you were away, Mrs. Hall let me in. Besides, I know your size as well as I know my own. Here, I hope it will do on the ship. The length looks alright."

"Alright… Fiona, it's perfect! I don't know how you did it." Chloe took the pink dress and held it up, noting with satisfaction the lace cuffs on the sleeves, and bodice. The waist was high with soft pleats falling into place on the narrow skirt. It was elegant in its simplicity and the pale pink silk would complement Chloe's fair skin and honey toned hair. "I had no idea you could sew like this. The sleeves are simply adorable." She said admiring the stylishly shortened sleeves.

"Oh, it's not much Chloe; I found the wonderful material while you were gone and was inspired. My aunt had given me this lace some time ago and I hadn't decided what to do with it. It was good luck that you bought those new shoes last weekend."

"So that's why you were so eager for me to buy those. But you're right they will look lovely with the dress. Oh Fiona, I don't know how to thank you." Chloe looked up endearingly at her friend.

"Please Chloe, it was my pleasure, and you will get many uses out of this dress, I imagine." Happening to glance over at the glassy stares of Hank and James, Fiona tugged on Hank and hastened to give her friend a good tight hug. "Don't you do falling in love with a tall dark stranger, now." She whispered so that only Chloe could hear and gave a knowing glance in James' direction.

Chloe couldn't think of a reply to that, so she only hugged Fiona tightly and promised to write about all of her experiences. Politely she shook hands with Hank who gave her an oddly old fashioned half bow. He tucked Fiona's arm firmly in his with an air of quiet pride and with a last wave Chloe saw them to the door. She watched them walk quickly down the street, staccato footsteps echoing in the sultry night. Closing the door on them, she found James standing with his coat ready, watching her with a heartwarming expression.

"What time is the carriage coming, Chloe?" He asked.

"Seven o'clock. Mrs. Mainthswaite likes to be punctual." She chuckled.

"I imagine so. Well, Chloe, I should like to come say goodbye beforehand if that's alright by you."

"Yes of course. I think I will be feeling quite homesick by the time I reach the dock."

"No," James gave her that smile which always made her stomach turn a slow somersault. "You'll be just fine Chloe. It's us who will miss you. I can't tell you how happy I am that you came back. I haven't said as much, but I am."

"I was always going to come home James, but I think that a prod from my sister helped me to see it faster, that's all. I was very worried about her." She met his eyes as she said it and was glad of the returned warmth.

"I know." With a gentle squeeze on her arm he was gone, and she shut the door on him with a feeling of contentment. The night had been filled with friends and laughter, and although it left Chloe feeling as though she might just rather stay home than go, she knew once she was on her way to the dock, it would be all she would think about. She lay awake in bed for some time thinking about the last few weeks of cooler behavior from James, and then tonight's sudden rekindling of tenderness in his eyes. She was not quite sure what had happened, but she felt more settled about her own feelings at least, that battle had ended when she was back home. Chloe had always assumed that one day she may meet someone to share her innermost thoughts and passions with, but had been determined not to settle for one who was merely agreeable. Naturally she had been quite unprepared to find herself face to face with such strong feelings so soon after establishing herself in New York. It was a bit alarming, yet exhilarating. She had a feeling that James too was battling with some of the same thoughts as she remembered the look in his eyes this evening. Nothing had been said by either party although Chloe realized now how strong the feelings must have grown in the time they had known each other. She had been by far too timid and conflicted to say anything, and once she resolved her decisions, he confused her with his behavior of late. Chloe hoped that he would soon say what lay in his heart rather than leave her guessing, and she hoped even more fervently that it was the same as what lay in hers. Finally after many such thoughts, she fell into a fitful sleep, waking up more than a few times to check the time.

Finally morning came. It was still quite dark, but Chloe knew she could not spend one more minute attempting to sleep when she was far too excited. She felt nervous and scared and happy all at once. Wondering how small and provincial she would seem among the ladies and gentlemen who made a practice of travelling, Chloe rose and dressed carefully in her favorite suit. She wished she had time to purchase a hat beforehand, but undoubtedly it would be much more fun to find one in London . Carefully folding the beautiful dress from Fiona in her battered trunk which had taken her many miles from her hometown and would now see the shores of a distant land, she heaved it closed and sat down by the window to watch and wait.

James knocked on the front door a little before the carriage was to come. She had seen him from her window and hastened down the stairs so as not to rouse the rest of the household. He followed her up into her room which already had a bare empty feeling. She perched on the trunk and tried to engage in light conversation but found herself too nervous and excited to do much more than fiddle with the clasp of her small carryall bag.

James fumbled with something he had brought, asking her if she had brought her journal.

"Of course I have, that was the first thing I packed." Chloe laughed. "You know I can't do without it."

"Yes I do know that, that's why I brought you this." He held out a small red leather book with a silk strap to hold it closed.

She took the book with a gasp of delight and opened it, riffling its enticingly blank lined pages. "It's beautiful James. This will be my special journal for only this trip. Thank you. It's just wonderful."

He grinned sheepishly. "I'm glad you like it. I wanted you to have a special one for this adventure. This is a dream come true for you."

He glanced out of the window as a scrape of wheels announced the arrival of Mrs. Mainthswaite's carriage. "Well, here is your carriage." He held out a hand to help her up from the trunk.

"Thank you. I have to get the trunk down and my carryall. Fortunately I have no other luggage." Chloe made as if to move toward the door as she heard a knock but James blocked her way. Heart thumping, she gazed at James for a few long moments as the driver knocked again impatiently at the door. Without knowing quite how it happened, Chloe found herself swept up in James arms and felt his arms tighten around her for one delicious minute that seemed to last forever. Quickly, his lips brushed hers ever so softly that Chloe was afraid she had imagined it, and then he was gone, striding down the stairs with her trunk before she realized what happened. She gathered up her hat and her small bag, and left the room, after surveying it one last time. Her body was numb and her heart racing from the embrace, she knew not how to react. Squaring her shoulders when she reached the ground, she decided to take decisive action. She marched up to the carriage, deposited her bag and hat on the seat and swiveled around to James. Taking his hands in hers she smiled up at him, and quite boldly for her, stood up on tiptoe to give him a soft kiss on the corner of his mouth. Reaching up to brush a lock of stray hair out of his eyes, she said, "I'll be thinking of you every day. I know I will." In response James tightened his grasp on her hands and they stayed like that for another moment, relishing the closeness and tingle of electricity racing between them. She reluctantly let go of his hands and climbed into the carriage as the driver coughed insistently. Encouraged by this movement, the driver quickly set the horses into a quick trot, perhaps afraid that Chloe would impulsively leap from the carriage. She stuck her head out of the window and waved to James, watching him grow smaller as the carriage made its way down the busy street. She sat back against the cushions, a smile spreading across her face, and remained in a golden haze all the way to Mrs. Mainthswaite's house.

Chapter 16

Bright sunlight streamed into the small round window, sparkling as it bounced off the sea salt that had blown onto the window, little diamonds of light making Chloe squint . The discreet knock sounded again and a maid entered on Chloe's acknowledgement, depositing a tray on the end of her bed. The soft voice murmured that it was from her employer, and withdrew, leaving the silver tray with its steaming beverage and plate of delicate pastries. Chloe tossed aside her covers and made as if to spring out of bed, remembering just in time the heaving ship would almost certainly unsteady her. She was still learning to cope with the rolling of the ship after two days. Slowly moving, to give her legs time, she got up and crossed the tiny room to her wardrobe, wrapping herself in her ancient robe, and helped herself to breakfast. Chloe knew that if she endeavored to make such a trip, she would never be able to afford such posh accommodations and treatment. The cabin was tiny, half the size of Mrs., Mainthswaite's, in fact it was hardly meant for a true cabin. Mrs. Mainthswaite had insisted, however, that Chloe adjoin her cabin and, being the influential person she was, the company had complied as best they could. Despite the size however, the furnishings were mahogany and the down comforter was soft. Chloe was not able to express her gratitude to Mrs. Mainthswaite who had waved her stammered thanks aside with a wave of one of her elegantly gloved hands. Chloe relished the quiet of the morning, hearing occasional footsteps in the hall and the sounds of voices out on deck. Her tiny cabin had only a small round window, merely for light, but that was fine for Chloe. She finished her breakfast at leisure, knowing that her duties would not begin in earnest until mid-morning. Mrs. Mainthswaite had spent the last two mornings strolling along the deck enjoying the vigorous sea air and making the acquaintance of other of her peers. She did not call for Chloe until ten o'clock. After dressing in a light skirt and wrapping her shawl around herself against the breezy air on deck, Chloe made her way to the nearest part of their deck and leaned against the railings, as she had discovered that she loved to do, just breathing in the salty air and feeling the wind against her face. Having grown up far from the sea, it still entranced her to walk near the water in New York. To be surrounded by the sparkling blue vastness of the ocean was quite overwhelming but she loved it.

Once again immersed in her duties, Chloe shut out the noises she heard and concentrated on the work at hand, at least for the day time hours. The evenings had proved thus far to be both entertaining and very daunting. Chloe had felt all of her small town upbringing must show on her face when she first stepped through the double doors into the grand dining room. Mrs. Mainthswaite's sardonic remarks did nothing to dispel Chloe's wonderment at the opulence of the first class areas of the ship. The dining room was a large rectangular room, glittering with chandeliers which caught tiny rainbows of light in the crystal. Gleaming white cloths graced the many tables with their array of silverware and china. On her first evening, Chloe found to her dismay that they shared the table with several other first class passengers, all looking as elegant and well-travelled as Mrs. Mainthswaite. Chloe had sat in her seat, trying to be invisible and whispered polite replies when spoken to. Two days later Chloe could now look upon that first night with a shudder, but after becoming acquainted with her fellow diners, she was eager to finish her duties this afternoon. Quite unaccountably, a matronly looking woman of middle age had taken Chloe under her wing and had endeavored to break her out of her shell. She had made sure to introduce Chloe to other passengers, many of whom seemed quite familiar with each other. Chloe never realized quite how small society was. Chloe's new found friend was a Mrs. Hyacinth Wiggenham, a very wealthy and well known woman apparently who lived in New York, not too far from the grand houses of Mrs. Mainthswaite's neighborhood. She was an interesting and kindly woman and had done her best to make Chloe comfortable among the glittering jewels and elegant suits of the upper class. Chloe found herself drawn to Mrs. Wiggenham not only for her candid and motherly nature but also because, in spite of her wealth, she was never able to deport herself quite as elegantly as per other peers. Hyacinth always seemed to have rather too many shawls draped around her generous frame which needed to constantly be picked up and her faded red curls were determined to escape their many hair pins. This made Chloe feel slightly less provincial in her plain green dress which she herself had made, even if it was dressed up with a lovely lace wrap of Mrs. Mainthswaite's and Chloe's mother's pearl necklace. After that night, Hyacinth was wont to collect Chloe each day in early evening, after she was done with Mrs. Mainthswaite, and promenade on the deck, in the cool air with Chloe's arm tucked under her own ample one. Hyacinth regaled Chloe with fascinating stories from her youth or extolled the virtues of her two lovely daughters to such an end that Chloe had decided they must be quite amazing indeed. Chloe was highly entertained by these reminiscences and loved to hear about Hyacinth, as she demanded Chloe call her. It gave Chloe a real insight into human nature and she found much meat for her own literary endeavors. These late afternoon strolls among the groups of young ladies flirting coyly under their mother's stern eyes, and the sun dipping so that it made the sea gleam, were probably Chloe's favorite part of the cruise.

"Chloe, my girl, you should have seen the parties that we had at our cottage back in my younger days. My, they were fun. If only Jonnie were still alive, he would have loved another sea voyage. He was always such a traveler." Hyacinth prattled on, leaving Chloe for the memories of years past, when her husband was alive and they travelled the globe. Chloe listened, caught up in visions of twenty years past. This was the third night on the ship, almost the midpoint of the journey. After seeing Hyacinth back to her large stateroom, Chloe quickly made her way back to her own to get ready for dinner.   She dressed as elegantly as she could, in her best suit and heavy ivory silk blouse. She was glad of the new shoes that Fiona had enticed her to buy. All of the other girls of her age sported glistening jewels and silk gowns draped enticingly with narrow skirts to show their silk clad ankles. Chloe knew that by now no one could mistake her for anything other than Mrs. Mainthswaite's companion and assistant so she did not attempt to look stylish when she could not. She did however have the beautiful dress which Fiona had presented to her on her last night before leaving, but she was saving that for the last dinner on the ship which would be the most formal. She did up her hair in pearl tipped pins which Fiona had lent her and paired that with her pearl necklace and found the effect to be very satisfactory. She walked into the dining room, following Mrs. Mainthswaite in her elegant gunmetal gray dress. Soft music swirled around them and the indistinct sounds of laughter and tinkling china blended together. Swirls of pinks and blues, lace and silks fluttered by as other girls of the first class flitted their eyed coquettishly and, in Chloe's opinion, annoyingly in any eligible male's direction. What with her new realization of what James meant to her, plus the complete foolishness of finding a soul mate at sea, Chloe endeavored to present a neat and pretty appearance, and to enjoy herself most of all. She found it entertaining to observe this self-involved and very close knit example of high society. The dinner tonight was delicious. The delicate chicken, vegetables which boasted a freshness that made it hard to believe they had not been picked that day, lovely sherbet. The food that the people around her took for granted, Chloe savored and reminded herself that more than once a week she herself had been accustomed to skipping dinner and grazing on bread and cheese. After dinner, people tended to mingle in the music saloon. Introductions were made, or even, it seemed, business meetings arranged. Mrs. Wiggenham had been buttonholed by a loud woman in a rusty lace outfit which was completely wrong for her figure, and had gone off apologetically, leaving Chloe to herself sitting in one of the comfortable wing backed chairs. She was happy to sit and quietly observe when she heard a clearing of a throat and looked up to behold one of the elderly gentlemen from her dining table, Major Stears standing by her chair.

"Chloe, my dear, may I trouble you for an introduction." Standing slightly behind the Major was a handsome young man smiling quite blandly at Chloe. She gave an undecided nod, uncertain as to whether the Major had taken it upon himself to play matchmaker or if this young man had asked for an introduction. The chiming of crystal and the laughter of the guests enjoying the music following dinner made a fitting background against this young man's obviously fashionable suit. He seemed to know he cut quite a dashing figure among the company. She stood, smiling politely and murmured that she would be pleased to make his acquaintance.

"This is Mr. Landall Jones. He is on his way to England for business. This is his first trip to sea as well." The Major looked from one to the other, pleased, as if having never been on a ship before would make her a lifelong friend to Mr. Jones.

"Please call me Landall, or just Lands, everyone does." The young man drawled in pleasantly bored tones. "So nice to meet you, er, Chloe. Won't you take some refreshment?" Here Mr. Jones offered his elbow and the Major, having successfully delivered Mr. Jones out of his company, left. Chloe gave an inward sigh and accepted the glass of wine with an air of resignation. On the far side of the room, Chloe spotted Mrs. Mainthswaite. The elder lady glanced incredulously at Landall, who was talking nonstop. Chloe raised her eyebrows and speechlessly implored her employer to call upon her in a short time.

Landall stopped his monologue and remembered his guest. "Ah Chloe, pretty name. And what brings you on this voyage?" He leant against the wall elegantly; well aware of the glances he was awarded from other young women in their vicinity.

"I am a companion, and a secretary to Mrs. Mainthswaite." Chloe was hoping that the name meant something to him and she was not disappointed. She continued, noting his raised eyebrows. "I'm a writer as well."

"Oh, er, how nice for you." Landall said awkwardly, fumbling for something else to speak about, as Chloe watched amused at the knowledge that he probably did not know any women who worked for a living. Hastily Chloe finished her wine, grimacing slightly at the bitter taste that she was not used to, and saw her employer making her way over. Muttering how pleased she had been to meet Mr. Jones and that she hoped to renew their acquaintance at another time, she fled toward her rescuer, as it were.

"Good Lord Chloe, who was that young man." Mrs. Mainthswaite directed her steely stare toward the unfortunate young man who flushed uncomfortably and made a hasty retreat toward the doors leading to the smoking room, evidently a place where more of his peers had gathered. She took Chloe by the arm and steered her in the opposite direction out toward the passageway to the first class state rooms, much to Chloe's great relief.

Chloe explained that the introduction had been made by Major Stears. She did not want to give Mrs. Mainthswaite any reason to find fault with her, however the perceptive older lady could see plainly that Chloe was very relieved indeed to have been extricated from what could have been a very dull night. Mrs. Mainthswaite acknowledged Chloe's explanation with a definitive "hmpf" and directed that they retire to their beds early for the next day she wanted to get an early start. This advice was taken with alacrity; however Chloe didn't retire just then. The moon was almost full, and Chloe could see it shining through the tiny window in her cubbyhole of a room. It was quite bright and flooded the room with a pale cold light which was unlike that in the city with its many artificial lights. Chloe perched on her bunk for a long time that night, looking at the moon and the bright stars which were the same as the ones shining over the city tonight. She imagined that perhaps James was looking at them as well, and perhaps thinking of her. She pulled out her journal, the special gift that James had given her, holding it for a moment and breathing in the scent of its leather cover. Then she wrote. She wrote for a long time about different characters she had met on the ship. And then thought perhaps she would try a new exercise. Perhaps she might try writing some fiction. A short story perhaps. Her sister Mary had long been the authority on poetry, everyone in the family knew that, while she entertained her brothers with her descriptions of true life. Perhaps she would mix fact and fiction and come up with an amusing anecdote taking place on this very ship. With this enticing thought, she fell into a dreamless sleep.

    The next morning dawned in a cloudless burst of splendor, and true to her word, Chloe was awakened by a summons from Mrs. Mainthswaite, who bade her to sit and eat. Then she directed Chloe to take notes for their imminent arrival in England. In just about three days they would arrive and from there travel to London for several weeks with a shorter stay in Paris. Mrs. Mainthswaite, having seen all there was to see in the two great cities, was planning several excursions for the benefit of Chloe. She knew that unless circumstances changed drastically Chloe would not be able to afford such a trip, therefore by assuring Chloe that her secretarial acumen was necessary, both women were able to get the most from the coming trip. As well as business, there were some family members and old friends and colleagues of Mrs. Mainthswaite's husband that she intended to call upon. Chloe was happily immersed in these plans for the remainder of the morning. Mrs. Mainthswaite was an excellent employer, Chloe thought to herself, not for the first time. She was strict and exact, but to be fair, generous perceptive and highly intelligent. Chloe found herself admiring the older woman more and more the better she came to know her.

The day passed quickly, letters to be sorted and certain business papers needed to be filed appropriately. In no time, it was past noon and Mrs. Mainthswaite announced that she had sent for some sandwiches. They worked another hour and then stopped for the day. Mrs. Mainthswaite decided that she would stroll on deck for a time and then retire to the ladies boudoir for the remainder of the afternoon. Upon being dismissed, Chloe spent some time curled on her bunk with her journal in which she wrote faithfully every day, making sure to record anything of interest in hopes that it might amuse her friends, especially James, who she thought of with unfortunate sentimentality the last few weeks. Chloe quickly banished the thoughts to the back of her mind, as she was still not quite comfortable with this new romantic part of herself which had forced its way into the open. Finally she pulled out another battered notebook that she had brought along and spent some time composing a short story. So drawn into this new endeavor she did not realize the time, and aroused by a knock from her friend Hyacinth, she rushed to dress for dinner as a dusky purple sky peeped in through the small round window. She walked with Hyacinth with a mild apprehension at the thought that the young man she had met the night before would be dancing attendance to her. A comforting thought occurred to her as she recalled how many other eyes were on him, and undoubtedly he would find more promising ears to confide in than hers.

    The waiters in their starched uniforms presented such a grand sight carrying the glittering crystal and china, whirling almost in time to the soft strains of the stringed quartet who played near her table. Chloe heartily enjoyed dinner, being highly entertained by Hyacinth on one side and a round small man on her other side who kept up such a stream of jokes as his wife unsuccessfully hid her embarrassment. After dinner, she and Hyacinth made their way to the lounge where a group of chattering young ladies had converged. Ignoring the main group, they sought out a quiet corner with two invitingly comfortable arm chairs. Unfortunately, she spotted Mr. Jones and quickly urged Hyacinth to stay by her side as the young gentleman made his way over to the two ladies. Hyacinth promised she would and with a look of distain resolutely ignored the pointed gesture for Chloe to accompany him to the other side of the lounge. Politely Hyacinth and Chloe listened as Landall, in an effort to impress Chloe perhaps, drawled incessantly about his whirlwind social life and grueling day at his father's firm. He repeatedly attempted to draw Chloe out to no avail. Chloe did not run in his circles socially and although, or perhaps because she seemed to be completely indifferent to his charms, he found her fascinating and so attempted to impress her with money. This worked even less than anything else. She had no wish to open up her wishes and dreams of working and writing to this decadent young man. Good looks notwithstanding, he could never understand her. Despite the grandeur of the room and the excitement of being on board a gigantic steamship, she heartily wished for the laughter and sympathetic soul she had found in James. Finally Chloe was rewarded when glancing surreptitiously at the tiny pendant watch she kept on her lapel at the request of Mrs. Mainthswaite, that it was a late enough hour to excuse herself and Hyacinth without appearing rude. Chloe had no interest in knowing Landall Jones, however there were three more days on board and she had no wish to antagonize him either. Graciously exclaiming that she needed to retire, she and Hyacinth bid Landall farewell with inward sighs of relief and quickly departed for their respective beds.

"Chloe that boy will make a fine husband one day, if his wife is deaf!" Hyacinth exclaimed as the two of them walked as quickly as was seemly. She stopped at the hallway to Chloe and Mrs. Mainthswaite's adjoining stateroom.

Chloe giggled. "Hyacinth, that is too bad of you. But true." With a final wave they went their separate ways. Chloe let herself into her tiny cabin, pausing to listen for signs that Mrs. Mainthswaite had already retired. The light was on in her room, so she deduced the older lady was relaxing after a full day. Quickly she jumped out of her clothes and bundled herself up into her warmest nightgown, climbing into the bunk with its wonderfully thick and warm blankets. "Not even three days left of this wonderful voyage." Chloe thought to herself. "And it's become a chore to socialize for fear of being bored silly." She shook her head and chided herself for such uncharitable thoughts. Perhaps he was merely showing off because he felt intimidated as well. But regardless of Landall and his incessant chatter, she would not let him ruin the remainder of the trip. They would be docking on the morning of the third and be off of the boat by midday. Tomorrow, Chloe determined, she would relax and enjoy the company of Mrs. Mainthswaite.

The next morning Chloe rose late. Since there was no summons from Mrs. Mainthswaite, Chloe lay in bed until her rumbling stomach told her that she needed to find some breakfast. Dressing quickly in a comfortable skirt and thick stockings, she knocked timidly on the adjoining door to Mrs. Mainthswaite's stateroom. It appeared that her employer was on the verge of leaving her room but she invited Chloe to partake of some extra pastries and coffee that had been ordered earlier. Chloe gratefully accepted and took the tray back to her room to enjoy.

Mrs. Mainthswaite poked her head back in, "Please feel free to join me in the library when you have finished. I hear they have quite a collection of magazines and periodicals." Chloe nodded her assent and Mrs. Mainthswaite withdrew. Chloe finished up her breakfast and quickly arranged her hair. It would get completely windblown once she stepped on deck of course. She spent an enjoyable few hours in the library, browsing through the shelves and chatting with other passengers. She and Mrs. Mainthswaite had a pleasant lunch and then Chloe, with nothing in particular to do, enjoyed a rare nap as the sunlight streamed into her cabin making motes of dust dance in the air. She later joined Hyacinth and strolled on the promenade deck noting the other couples in fine coats and shawls, enjoying the September sunshine. Undoubtedly the vacuous Mr. Jones had found another unfortunate young lady's ear to pour confidences into. The evening passed swiftly and pleasantly as well, and Chloe was sad that the voyage would soon be over; however she was excited as well. She couldn't wait to wear her lovely new dress for the last night's formal dinner.

The next day passed pleasantly as well. Chloe spent the afternoon with Hyacinth and a few other ladies she had become acquainted with. It was a breezy day again and the wind whipped up their skirts whenever they ventured on deck. For the most part people stayed indoors. After this pleasant afternoon however Chloe found the saloon had become stuffy and decided to walk along the deck despite the breeze. She wanted to savor the sun against the sea, since it would be October by the time they returned from England and no one would be enjoying the sea air. She found a quiet corner, not hard since most of the promenade deck was deserted, and leant against the wooden rail, breathing in the salty air. She felt that particular sense of sadness as the end of the voyage neared. Chloe's eyes had been opened in the past week to a whole new reality, but one that she didn't think she could feel at home with. Mrs. Mainthswaite moved among the rich old society families and the new wealth in their impeccable attire with an ease that Chloe knew she could never attain, nor did she want to. In this case she was content to be merely an observer of the tiny circle high society really was. Nevertheless she was still sad to see some acquaintances go, such as Hyacinth Wiggenham who had become a dear friend in a remarkable short time. She smiled ruefully to herself. "I didn't know any of these companions just a week ago, though it hardly seems possible, and here I am mourning their departure already as if they were lifelong companions." She laughed at her thoughts and squarely reminded herself that the end of the beautiful and exciting voyage was the beginning of a bigger adventure.

As the sun began its descent into the sea turning everything in its path golden and brilliant, her sweet yet melancholy thoughts were interrupted by an unfortunately familiar drawl behind her. Swinging around, she found herself face to face with none other than Landall Jones.

"Why Mr. Jones, how good to make your acquaintance again." Chloe stammered, aiming to be polite yet uninviting. Annoyingly shallow as he seemed, he was quite a good looking gentleman, Chloe reflected, as she swiftly glanced at his thick locks which had been ruffled by the wind. Too bad he knows it, she thought.

"Chloe, you act as if we are strangers. No good comes of being on such a grand ship by yourself." He offered Chloe his arm and after glancing around surreptitiously for any possible excuses not too, Chloe reluctantly assented. He wasn't giving her much of a choice, as he had firmly tucked her arm in his and was guiding her toward the promenade deck. "How many times have I asked you to call me Landall? We have no cause to be so formal, you and I."

Chloe murmured an apology and assure him she would call him Landall in future conversations. She asserted that her employer would likely be looking for her in a short time, but he laughed and told her he had seen Mrs. Mainthswaite in the music saloon earlier and didn't think she was going to need Chloe. As they walked down the deck with the waning sun bathing them in light that was so bright it almost leached the color out of the surroundings, she observed the studied nonchalance of the young men in their afternoon casual dress. Landall seemed to be a natural at this practice, and for the most part she let his conversation flow over her without disrupting her thoughts. Now and then however he hit upon an interesting topic and as they chatted she found herself warming up to him.

"Perhaps he is not so bad." Chloe thought. "He just needs to show his true self, instead of who he thinks he should be." She assumed in his society that it was hard to show your true personality and for a very small moment, pitied him. Chloe enjoyed herself somewhat until she realized with dismay that Landall had led her toward a more secluded area of the deck. It was one of several niches with a cluster of seats which were set so that an unobstructed view of the deepening blue sea could be enjoyed. He was now bemoaning the loneliness of being an only child and what trouble he had growing up. Chloe leant against the wide rail and said nothing. She thought about her own family and the camaraderie she had always felt with her sister and brothers and pitied him that, but did not feel much sympathy at his descriptions his large home and how empty it was. She gazed out at the water, now almost an indigo in parts where the setting sun did not quite reach. Its depths were mysterious and unsettling in their unfathomable expanse. Shed shivered involuntarily in the deepening chill. It was beginning to get quite cold out in the open with the wind blowing ceaselessly as evening was nearing. Suddenly the voice which had been emanating from one of the chairs upon which Landall indolently lounged was much closer, somewhere behind her left ear. She felt warmer as he draped his jacket over her shoulders, but her gratitude was tempered with dismay at his voice being uncomfortably close.

"Ah Chloe, you look quite chilled, I suppose we should be heading inside soon. We don't want you to catch a cold. "But Landall made no effort to move from her side. "Chloe, I would very much like you to accompany me to the dinner tomorrow. As it's our last night on board." His hand lightly covered one of hers and remained that way.

"Mr. Jones," Chloe said firmly with an emphasis on the formal address. "My employer Mrs. Mainthswaite will surely insist on me joining her as our usual arrangement. She will be most insistent on that." She hoped her formal attitude would dissuade any further intimations of friendship on his part. "It was kind of you to ask." She added quickly, for however irritating he had been, she could not bring herself to be too hard on him. However naive Chloe was, she had not lived the better part of two years in a city teaming with all walks of life not to recognize what kind of man Landall was, and she was not taken in by his crestfallen expression. He may think that he was one of a kind, yet there were a dozens of young men and old just like him right on this ship. That Landall had not found Chloe to be acquiescent of his wishes was of no importance because he was not looking for companionship of the permanent kind right now.

"My dear, you overestimate your employer, surely on the last night she will not require your services. I'm sure she will gladly relinquish you into my company for I believe she knows my family."

"I do not think that would be appropriate. She has been so kind that I would not want to take advantage of her generosity."

"Chloe you must not let your charming diffidence get in the way of what could be a close friendship," Landall's voice was oily and overly solicitous in her ear. "Why, we have only these two last night's left on board. The last dinner always brings out the best of us, I am told. Let us enjoy this magnificent ship together. I can see how it agrees with you, or is it my company that makes you blush so." Landall teased, "Why, I have yet to see any girl who compares to you."

Chloe felt a hand lower to her waist and sidestepped deftly to avoid the other hand that was brushing away a wisp of her hair which had fallen across her cheek in the sea breeze. Whatever Chloe's opinion of her appearance, she had no delusions of great beauty. In no way did she compare herself to Fiona's snapping dark eyes and heavy mahogany hair, yet she was satisfied at her small expressive face which looked out under honey toned curls with gray green eyes. She inched slightly down the rail, widening the distance between herself and Landall. Really, what would Fiona say to this impudent young man making assumptions that were clearly not the case? How they would laugh about this episode during one of their cozy confabs in the dingy room which Chloe rented. Chloe felt as acute sense of homesickness stab her heart like a needle, which she had not yet experienced in the excitement of the journey. All of her adventurous feelings faded and she heartily wished she were back in that beloved room with its rusty brass bedstead and streaked window. Indeed she would trade all of the opulence of this grand ship for her close friends in the city without a second thought. Most of all she simply missed James. More than she ever had. Landall was observant enough at least to see that his sleek words were not having the desired effect. She was giving off the most formal air that she could as she looked at him steadily with more than a hint of frost in her green eyes. She stated coldly that she needed to return to her cabin as it was getting quite dark, and prepared to leave as his hand tightened momentarily on her arm. She was saved from his reply as an angel in the matronly guise of Hyacinth Wiggenham appeared.

"Chloe, my dear, where have you been? I've searched high and low for you. My goodness you're a hard one to find." After a silent prayer of thanks, Chloe bade a graceful apology to Landall for having to depart, and left Landall looking slightly crestfallen at having to find a new companion into which to pour his confidences. She hastily grasped Hyacinth by the arm and fairly dragged her back to the main deck.

"Chloe dearie, why in Heaven's name are you allowing that young layabout to paw you like that. My goodness, he has earned himself quite a reputation among the younger ladies and their hopeful mama's"

Chloe had not realized how eligible of a suitor Landall was, in trying to keep herself out of the midst of giggling and silly girls who generally crowded the promenade deck with their expensive and frivolous hats and lace. She had not considered him interesting enough to be eligible for anything, however she was well aware that he had his eye on every pretty girl who walked by him, even when in her company, which had proved most annoying.

Hyacinth chuckled at her surprised companion. "Don't go losing your head over the likes of him my dear, nothing will come of it, mark my words. Needless to say you would hardly be a perfect choice for his mother. Word has it that she is as picky as they come and no one is too good for her Landall.

Chloe laughed both for the sheer relief she found from her narrow escape and at the candidness of her friend who did not mince words in her honesty. Her high clear laugh echoed in the cold air causing several appreciative glances from stragglers who were still enjoying the dusky air. Chloe assured her friend that she had not the slightest dream of pursuing a friendship or anything more with the eligible Landall Jones.

"But what is it that you desired to speak with me about, Hyacinth? We have come off the topic."

Hyacinth let out a rather undignified snort of laughter and said. "Oh that? I was just trying to get you out of there."

"Well I dearly thank you for it Hyacinth. He is not as horrible as I had first thought, however I pity him for feeling such pressure to put on a façade. However much he thinks of himself, I do believe I have the better of him in spirit."

"That you do, dearie." Hyacinth gave Chloe's arm and affectionate squeeze and the two ladies continued down the deck following the last of their fellow passengers as they headed indoors to warmth and light. They parted at Hyacinth's stateroom. Chloe went to her own room which was warm and bright and cheerful. Out of her small round window, the sea shone dark and purple as the moon had not made itself visible over the water. Back in the quiet stillness, Chloe recounted, not without some amusement and a shudder or two, her recent activities in her special leather bound journal. She must remember to tell Fiona all about Landall as she was sure the two of them would have a grand time over this incident. She could almost see Fiona with her head thrown back in mirth as they imitated the drawling accents of Landall and the other snobbishly charming debutants which crowded the music and dining rooms. Chloe did not think this would be quite so amusing to James however and she would be more detailed on the descriptions of the ship and sea than on the people. She missed James more than she had anticipated at times like this when she was alone in her cabin, remembering their gay little picnics or walks in the park amidst the crowded buildings of the city. Most of the time, however, the heartache was something she pushed aside in her excitement. The ease of this alarmed her at times, but then her longing to see him would come flooding back reassuring her than she truly loved him and felt almost certain he did as well. It was that which that kept her up nights. She reread the pages that she had written in the past few days, so familiar in her small neat handwriting, then carefully closed the journal and tucked it away in her trunk to get ready for dinner.

The next day was full of a stifled excitement as the crew and passengers alike readied themselves for the last night on board. There was a flurry of activity in the main dining room and music saloon, and the decks were deserted soon after luncheon had ended so that the first class passengers could rest and prepare for the grand occasion. Chloe wondered about the lower decks. She had not been down there, although if she was not accompanying Mrs. Mainthswaite she would surely be one of the third class passengers. Chloe retired for some time to her cabin with the rest of the first class, more because of the stiff breeze which permeated most of the more open areas of the ship. After a time of quiet, Chloe heard rustling next door and presumed that Mrs. Mainthswaite had commenced her preparations for the night. Chloe took her time with her own toilet, brushing her hair until it shone pale honey curls under the dim light, and carefully stepping into the beautiful dress which Fiona had made. It was the fanciest thing Chloe had owned. She paired it with her mother's pearl beads which were always carefully preserved. A knock at the door interrupted Chloe's internal debate of how to wear her hair. Mrs. Mainthswaite poked her head in to ask if she was ready. Chloe nodded an assent, and hesitantly asked whether she should leave her hair down with a clip. Mrs. Mainthswaite regarded Chloe for a moment then decisively said "Put it up, In fact, I have a clip which would look lovely with that dress." Chloe followed Mrs. Mainthswaite into her room and obediently took the proffered clip, which would indeed look good. It was gold and very delicate, and as Chloe twisted her hair into it, Mrs. Mainthswaite held out two matching hair pins which would set it off perfectly. In addition, Chloe was pressed upon to take a beautiful pair of pearl drop earrings which could clip on to her ears. Since Chloe had not had the courage to pierce her ears, she was very excited about them. Mrs. Mainthswaite waved aside Chloe's enthusiastic gratitude with a wave of her elegantly ringed hand and the two set off for dinner.

"You look lovely Mrs. Mainthswaite," Chloe remarked as the two ladies made their way towards the dining room. Always elegantly attired, Mrs. Mainthswaite had outdone herself. Her pale gold dress was stylish yet appropriate for her age and station. The cloth was rich and set off the diamonds twinkling at her throat and in her regal silver hair. Mrs. Mainthswaite inclined her head, gave Chloe her tight smile and continued on toward her seat, skirt rustling. The dining room gleamed with an unusual brilliance as if the ship itself was aware of this last night, as if it was reminding Chloe to never forget the opulence and decadence for it might not show itself very often. The candles set on every table flickered gaily casting shadows on the gleaming silver and china. The menu was beyond the usual sumptuous fare and it seemed that, like Chloe and Mrs. Mainthswaite everyone was striving to outshine their seat partner. The dresses were fantastic and swirls of color, feathers, and silk surrounded them. Hyacinth bustled over as soon as she saw Chloe. She was handsomely dressed in a gown of deep lavender which unfortunately had a loose hem that kept getting stepped on. Hyacinth didn't seem to notice the trailing strip of material and soon had ensconced herself next to Chloe. Across the room Hyacinth saw Landall escorting a young woman with gleaming blond hair in a bright blue dress. She wore a self-satisfied expression as she clung to his arm. Chloe inclined her head toward him as he gave her a wink, no longer wary that she was in danger of giving mixed signals, she smiled openly. The evening went long past midnight as many of the guests gathered to listen to the stringed instruments and dance while the older generation sat in attendance and nodded off. Chloe enjoyed herself immensely as she passed the time chatting with Hyacinth and dancing with several young men she had met in passing during the evening.   Chloe dragged herself back to her cabin amid other giggling passengers to fall into her bunk almost instantly asleep, with the starlight peeping through her window shining dimly on her blankets.

Chapter 17

Cries of greedy seagulls woke Chloe to the early sunlight streaming through the cabin. Sitting up wearily and regretting momentarily the late night, Chloe rubbed her eyes and checked her tiny watch. Only six o'clock. Chloe sat back against her pillows for a while to reflect on the evening and indeed the whole voyage. It certainly had been a wonderful adventure so far, and they had not even reached their destination. Chloe knew they had docked, as the rolling movement was absent. Chloe felt that she had satisfied the requirements of her employer as well as enjoyed a whirlwind of activities which she knew she would not have a chance to in the future unless her living conditions changed drastically. Even the persistence of Landall was now fading into her memory and she was able to look at it with more amusement than previously. She looked forward London with great anticipation. She knew that her secretarial duties would be needed by Mrs. Mainthswaite but more so simply as a companion. Unlike many women of her same age and station, Mrs. Mainthswaite shunned the practice of travelling with a servant just for show. She had brought her housemaid Grace on several excursions to the country, however much more for Grace's amusement and experience than any need on Mrs. Mainthswaite's part. However stern and austere Mrs. Mainthswaite appeared, she was wont to give her household staff much more freedom and leisure time than most wealthy families would consider.

While listening to the thumps and thuds indicating the docking of the ship, Chloe also thought about the growing stack of pages in her red journal and knew that perhaps one day these pages would open doors she had only yet begun to dream about. She hoped that this trip would inspire her imagination, and help that dream of becoming a successful writer into a reality. Finally as her eyelids began to droop once again, a hard thump sounded out on deck which brought her fully awake. It was time to dress and make sure her belongings were all neatly stowed in her small trunk. She dressed quickly, the cold floor making her bare feet tingle. Glancing around the room, she reassured herself that she had packed all of her belongings, and knocked on Mrs. Mainthswaite's door. After receiving permission to enter, she brought her trunk and carryall and stepped over the sill into the much larger quarters. Mrs. Mainthswaite sat among her own trunks sipping coffee.

"Well girl, you have completed your first sea voyage, how about that." One of her rare crusty smiles brightened Mrs. Mainthswaite's stern visage. She indicated that Chloe sit at her small table and partake of the coffee and rolls which were on a silver platter. Chloe gratefully poured some of the steaming beverage and curled her cold hands around it trying to warm herself. "When you are done, please see that our trunks reach the porter successfully and give this to him." She handed Chloe a small envelope which Chloe took to be a small gratuity for the kindly porter, and turned back to her coffee. Chloe finished her coffee and roll in silence, quickly left to find the porter and instruct him on what to do with the trunks when leaving, which would not be for another few hours as the crew would be scurrying to and fro, busy with the docking of the majestic ship.

After finishing her duties as instructed by Mrs. Mainthswaite, Chloe returned to see that her employer had everything she needed. Chloe left her own battered carryall in her quarters as she would not need it for some time. Chloe made sure that any letters Mrs. Mainthswaite needed were easily accessible in the small satchel containing Mrs. Mainthswaite's business papers. Her employer had many acquaintances and business contacts in London and wished to schedule appointments once they were comfortably lodged in London. With this task done, Mrs. Mainthswaite declared she was going to remain indoors and read until it was time to disembark. Chloe however could not contain her excitement and decided to stroll out to the main deck and observe the activity below. Mrs. Mainthswaite waved her on indulgently and told her to 'have fun'.

Chloe was both nervous and exhilarated at the thought of seeing a different country for the first time. During the last few days, she had grown comfortable with life on the ship but her excitement was back and reminded her how intimidating and wonderful her journey to the city was so long ago. She thought of the trepidation she had felt at starting anew. This time however, she was merely gaining experience and travelling with the ease of someone much wealthier. She had left much of her anxiety behind once the first fear of the ship had left her, and relaxed in the knowledge that she had a wonderful and intelligent employer who could traverse the confusion of a new country with such ease that Chloe was left only with her excitement, and determination to glean every last bit of enjoyment from this trip.

The deck was a mass of people. Just about everyone on board was vying for a good spot, leaning over the rails in order to see the small figures below. The sun was deceptively bright today, but the cold breeze ruffled Chloe's hair and made her feel glad that there were so many people to block the wind. She drew her coat more tightly around her shoulders as she spotted her friend Hyacinth not too far along the rail, wedged between two rather stout men. They were all watching the scene below with the same excitement and animation that Chloe felt.

Chloe hastened over to where Hyacinth was standing with difficulty and inserted herself into a tiny space which Hyacinth made by giving one of the men a sharp nudge with her elbow. "I knew I would find you here Hyacinth, but what a crowd!"

"Naturally, dearie, it's the most exciting part. Well, this and the departure. I would have tracked you down anyway. Do you know where you are staying when you reach London?"

Chloe shook her head; the rough cloth of one of the gentlemen's scarves tickled her cheek, so close was the crowd. "Mrs. Mainthswaite has a pretty detailed itinerary. She is a very exact planner, but I don't know the name of anything just yet. I should do." Chloe laughed ruefully, "I have probably written it half a dozen times too. I am sure the hotel will be well appointed and very comfortable knowing Mrs. Mainthswaite."

Hyacinth laughed "If I know anything it will surely be posh even to my standards. Brr it's downright freezing out here. Would you like to watch the action from a more sheltered area?" Hyacinth pulled her voluminous wool shawl even closer and shivered so that the brim of her hat quivered; reminding Chloe of a large dog she had as a child.

Chloe didn't mind the chill terribly for September could be chilly at times, at least in New York and certainly Stuflen. The excitement of her first voyage was keeping her warm, however there really wasn't too much more to see besides to watch the little workers, carriages and cars swarming over the dock area in their numerous tasks. It would be at least another hour before the passengers would be able to disembark and that would most likely turn into quite a stampede. Chloe assented and together they fought through the crowd to find some chairs in a sheltered part of the promenade deck. The deck chairs which had been at such a premium on the warmer days of the journey had now been abandoned and stood forlornly along the wall as people preferred to lean over the railings and watch the scene below. The two sat comfortably, discussing the past few days and engaging in the age old practice of people watching until a slow movement of people indicated that the ship was now disgorging its waiting passengers who milled around in excited anticipation clutching purses and bags. Small children in their impeccable outfits accompanied by stern nannies poked their heads from between the railings only to be pulled back repeatedly, their light small laughing voices echoing among the scream of gulls and chatter of anxious matrons.

The movement along the deck signaled that it was time to depart from their cozy niche and go their separate ways; however Hyacinth accompanied Chloe back to her cabin so that the two friends could exchange addresses. Chloe was uncomfortably aware that she felt a distinct sadness at their goodbye. She had not realized she would find such a good friend in the slightly eccentric Hyacinth Wiggenham.

"Now don't you fret Chloe, why, I practically live next door, that's how close I am." Hyacinth had a lovely large house somewhere in the neighborhood where Mrs. Mainthswaite was, just a bit farther. Hyacinth patted Chloe's arm comfortingly. "We'll have a real good time when I come to visit you, you can bet on that!" With a wink and a motherly hug, Hyacinth was gone.

Chloe passed into Mrs. Mainthswaite's stateroom where her employer sat straight backed in her chair with the air of one who has seen the world. Chloe reflected as she sat in the opposite chair that Mrs. Mainthswaite probably had done just that.

"I see that the passengers are now departing the ship. I did not feel it was necessary to brave the crowd this time, but the porter was kind enough to knock as he passed and inform me that we would be able to disembark. Did you enjoy watching the activity? It's quite interesting isn't it how many tasks there are to dock the ship."

Chloe nodded eagerly and filled Mrs. Mainthswaite in on the interesting scenes she had witnessed. She knew Mrs. Mainthswaite had been on many trips and probably had seen all there was to see, but Chloe's own excitement was like a bubble of warm air and she could barely keep her feet on the ground. "The crowd by the rail is tremendous. I didn't know so many people were aboard! It was amazing." Chloe laughed out loud from happiness. Her excitement was so contagious that Mrs. Mainthswaite concealed her own smile with difficulty. "Shall we wait for a bit until the majority of the crowd has dispersed?" Chloe knew that Mrs. Mainthswaite had little patience with most of her peers and would prefer to wait for a while. Mrs. Mainthswaite nodded her approval at this and calmly reached for her book again.

"You are right Chloe; in fact, our transport would only just be arriving. Let us wait for a good half hour."

Chloe knew that Mrs. Mainthswaite had made arrangements to hire an automobile in order to convey them to London. This would be yet another milestone for Chloe. She had ridden in one on the rare occasion before, but to be treated to such a ride in a fancy black one such as those she had seen in pictures would be lovely. Chloe waited impatiently, casting surreptitious glances at Mrs. Mainthswaite's silver head as it bent over her book. Finally it was decided that they depart and Mrs. Mainthswaite packed away her book and indicated that Chloe precede her to the deck. The salty fishy smell in the air greeted them as they finally emerged from the ship amongst a vast number of people, some in similar clothes as Mrs. Mainthswaite right alongside many whom Chloe would call her own peers, with the same warm serviceable garb. The shiny automobile was parked exactly where Mrs. Mainthswaite was directed by one of the harried looking porters and in no time their trunks were loaded and they were ensconced in the deep plush seats. The driver acknowledged them with a tip of his cap and they set off without ceremony. Chloe only had time to glance back at the ship, floating amongst the others like a majestic queen, and it was gone. She watched with interest as the buildings began to slip by. Mrs. Mainthswaite started to fill Chloe in on some facts about London that she might find interesting. But try as she might, Chloe could not keep her eyelids from closing. Soon the jolting of the road went unnoticed by her as her head rested against the back. Mrs. Mainthswaite gave her a look of unexpected tenderness, something Chloe would not have seen had she been awake, and sat gazing out at the scenery that she had known so well as a younger woman.

Chapter 18

Shaken gently back to consciousness by Mrs. Mainthswaite, Chloe opened her eyes, yawned widely, and looked around with interest. The car was not any less jolty or noisy, yet the buildings now slipping by were reminiscent of her own city. The streets flashed by, but Chloe had impressions of stone and brick, of sidewalks wet with a newly fallen rain. The buildings looked like businesses but soon it became clear that they had reached their destination as they pulled to a stop in front of a stone hotel. Its elegance was irrefutable. It was by far the grandest building that Chloe had ever stepped foot in. She entered the vast lobby and looked around as Mrs. Mainthswaite gave her name. The hotel was not old, according to Mrs. Mainthswaite, but it had a timeless quality to it which would have served it well in any time period Chloe could imagine. There were tables and chairs scattered about the room, occupied by those of obviously more wealth than Chloe could ever hope to achieve. Elegant columns emphasized the ornate ceilings and Chloe felt like a bit like a child as she stood and took in every bit while trying not to gape. Chloe felt a tug at her sleeve bring her back to reality and she followed her Mrs. Mainthswaite's straight back to their room, the older lady barely glancing at the wondrous scenes. Again Chloe's smaller room adjoined Mrs. Mainthswaite's. Indeed it was more likely simply a dressing room, tastefully appointed, which had been converted upon Mrs. Mainthswaite's request. It suited Chloe just fine however and Mrs. Mainthswaite's room included a round table and two chairs as well as a small desk which would be perfect for Chloe's secretarial work. The broad window overlooked the busy street several stories below. At once Chloe felt the excitement set in from such an eventful day. Although eager to explore the hotel, Mrs. Mainthswaite felt that Chloe would not appreciate its grandness until she settled in and had a good night sleep to make up for the night before. Although not the least bit tired, Chloe excused herself from Mrs. Mainthswaite and closed the door gently on the outside world. The room contained everything Chloe might need, and after opening her trunk and moving a few things into the tall wardrobe, she shrugged into her comfortable and completely faded nightgown, crawled into bed and spent the next few hours examining every inch of the city from her window and writing it all down before falling into a fitful sleep.

The light filtering through the drawn curtains woke Chloe at an unknown hour. It was light enough that she could see through the gloom of early morning. For a moment she forgot completely where she was, and wondered that she was so used to the rolling of the boat that she didn't even notice anymore. Then as she lay among the down pillows, the docking and trip to London came back to her as sleep reluctantly left. Once she felt fully awake and refreshed, regardless that morning had not fully dawned, she sat up, pushing aside the burgundy colored curtains to peer out at the street, so different looking in the misty morning. Her room adjoined Mrs. Mainthswaite's which was at the end of the long hallway, so her smaller window looked out on a side street. The street below was quiet, and Chloe surmised that much like New York, it was not as busy as the working class neighborhoods, which was where she was more comfortable. The air was gray and a fine mist was like a veil on the window. Turning her head and squinting into the foggy street, she could just make out what looked like a square or park at the end of the cross street. After some time spent trying to make out all the little details on the facing buildings, Chloe decided to dress and set her room to rights since last night she did the very minimum. She chose her blue skirt and a plain blouse since she wasn't sure what the day would bring but decided that would be presentable and comfortable. Once she had put everything in its place, she surveyed the small neat room with its washbasin and wardrobe and bed in matching dark wood. Glancing at her pendant watch which she found still pinned to her pink dress, she saw that it was now after seven o'clock and while she was unsure of the workings of a hotel, her stomach announced that it needed food immediately. Last night the ladies had supped on a very light meal after their journey ended in London. Chloe found a bell pull near the door with which she could order some breakfast. Unsure of what to order when the maid arrived, she faltered for a moment at the knock on the door. A pert maid in a crisp uniform stood outside waiting patiently. Her cool glance appraised Chloe and her shabby trunk and noted the uncertainly on Chloe's face. Undoubtedly she was more used to people of Mrs. Mainthswaite's social standing.

"P'rhaps some tea and scones miss?"

"Yes please" Chloe stammered out and then remembering Mrs. Mainthswaite asked if she would bring the same for the next room. The maid nodded approvingly and shut the door with a decisive snick. Perhaps she was imagining Chloe to be a travelling companion to the older lady, which wasn't far from the truth. After plumping the pillows on her bed Chloe returned to her post by the window and waited for breakfast while looking down into the brightening street which was now becoming more populated. She saw business men emerging from other buildings in their dark suits, and carriages and automobiles traversing the broad avenue in the front of the hotel. Sitting on the edge of her bed and gazing out at the bustle in this new yet familiar scene, she was barely aware that her employer had tapped on her door and now stood half in the doorway.

"Good morning Chloe, It's good to see you awake. Did you have a good night?" The older lady stood ramrod straight, sensibly dressed in a tweed skirt and blouse. Her silver hair was coiled as neatly as usual and an elegant broach rested against the high neck of her ivory blouse.

"Yes, thank you Mrs. Mainthswaite. The bed is quite comfortable."

Mrs. Mainthswaite smiled tightly and muttered something about the joys of a young back but just then a knock announced breakfast and Chloe was saved from asking her employer to repeat herself. Having graciously indicated that they set the table up in Mrs. Mainthswaite's room, the ladies settled down to delicious fresh baked scones and hot strong tea. Although Chloe preferred coffee, she was happy for any hot beverage. "Thank you for having the foresight to order breakfast Chloe. I must admit that although we had dinner, I find myself in need of a good breakfast. It must be the travelling. What do you think of our hotel so far?"

Chloe stopped to butter a second scone before answering enthusiastically. "I love it Mrs. Mainthswaite. It's beautiful."

"I'm glad, Chloe. Now on to the business for the day, I do have several appointments that I am hoping to accomplish today. I also send out a telegram and am awaiting a response from an old family friend and business associate of my late husbands. He has helped me to manage several of Edward's business interests and as soon as I receive his reply, we will determine the rest of the day. Naturally you must be eager to see some of the city as well.

Chloe was surprised by Mrs. Mainthswaite's verbal onslaught as the older lady was generally not talkative, but she assented to the day's order and assured Mrs. Mainthswaite that although she would love to see the sights, she would be happy to do so at Mrs. Mainthswaite's convenience. As the two ladies finished breakfast Chloe listened to the brief outline Mrs. Mainthswaite gave her on some of the interesting historical facts of the city. Then Chloe assisted her employer in some minor secretarial duties for the remainder of the morning, the sun finally deigning to make an appearance. Chloe thought longingly about the sights which were awaiting her, but firmly turned her mind to her work. She was rewarded not long after when the anticipated message appeared for Mrs. Mainthswaite and she announced that they would walk to the interview, since it would be nice for Chloe to see some of the sights on the way. As they left Mrs. Mainthswaite cast an appraising glance at Chloe as they prepared to depart and advised her to bring a shawl in case the air was chillier than Chloe was used to for early September. Chloe scurried to do as she was bid and they emerged on the mild day.

It was not a long walk but they took their time, Mrs. Mainthswaite pointing out interesting buildings along the way. Chloe thought it was a beautiful area of the city, and though she was sure there were just as many areas of mazelike tenements and working class neighborhoods as in New York, she felt it easy to forget that and pretend. The old gray stone building that Mrs. Mainthswaite sought stood magnificent in its worn elegance in the watery sunlight. It was quite intimidating though and Chloe felt every inch of her provincial upbringing as she hurried up the worn stone steps and through the graceful arched doorway behind Mrs. Mainthswaite. They stopped at a desk where Mrs. Mainthswaite spoke to a young man in somber attire. He motioned them forward and led them down a long hall, past several doors of gleaming mahogany paneling. They stopped near the end of the hall and he knocked and opened the door standing back to allow them to pass. All this was done with no more than a murmured good day. An elegant looking gentleman of about Mrs. Mainthswaite's age came forward from where he had evidently been sitting behind a massive desk. He was tall and slender with silver hair and a neat moustache.

"Elizabeth my dear, what a complete pleasure it is to see you again. Far too long in coming." He bowed deeply at them both, taking Mrs. Mainthswaite's hand, and then turned to Chloe bowing again in such an old fashioned manner that Chloe stifled a giggle. "And this is your assistant I presume? It is very good to meet you young lady."

Mrs. Mainthswaite made introductions and Chloe smiled politely as shyness overcame her. "Chloe this is Mr. Haydon. He is an old friend and business associate." She smiled quite warmly at Mr. Haydon who ushered them both to sit in deep leather armchairs. Chloe let her gaze wander about the room as the two old friends took a detour down memory lane dropping names and dates which Chloe was quite unfamiliar with, save for the occasional one she had come upon while organizing Mrs. Mainthswaite's correspondence. It was a large square masculine room, richly appointed with warm paneling and expensive looking carpets. Thick curtains muffled the noises from the streets and a cheerful fire crackled in the grate bringing the temperature of the room close to stifling. Brass gleamed and old leather tomes lined the walls. As Chloe relaxed in the comfortable atmosphere her thoughts fell upon her two friends' in New York. She found herself wondering what they would make of the city. It was so far away, but with many similarities, which probably held true for many cities. Particularly she longed for James's opinion. With the last few days of excitement she had not much time to think of him except for a warm feeling of comfort, but now she could picture him quite clearly, his brilliant eyes and quirky grin would say everything. She knew well that James was not a fan of such opulence, but he would dearly love this office with its shelves of books. Chloe turned her thoughts fully to James. What was he doing right now? She hoped he had good luck in his search for a new employment opportunity. He had certainly seemed busy the last few weeks before her trip. Indeed they had barely seen each other until that last night and morning, when she thought she made it clear what her feelings for him were. She could feel the heat rising to her cheeks and tried to banish the thought, however a sudden stab of longing pierced her as she thought about how much longer she would be away from him. The longing disturbed her in its intensity, and Chloe was afraid she would become one of those silly girls hanging on a man's every word. Not she! She was far too independent, but in the face of such strong feelings for James, her resolve crumbled and she felt herself wishing more than anything he was with her in this bright cheerful and elegant room. All at once, Chloe realized she had been so far away that she had been spoken to more than once. With a guilty start she wrenched herself back to the pleasant office and attended firmly to reality with a resolution to keep her heart away from her head.

"...are you Chloe?" Blushing Chloe murmured something that could be taken for a reply to a question which she hadn't heard. Mr. Haydon chuckled "Woolgathering I suppose. I am sorry, my dear, we seemed to have gotten away from the present. That happens with old friends you know." He winked at Mrs. Mainthswaite, who brought out the warmest smile Chloe had ever seen on the older lady's face. "Come, let's show you around the old place, keep you from getting bored silly."

Taking the arm proffered, Chloe assured Mr. Haydon that she had not been the slightest bit bored, and hoping fervently that her thoughts had not shown on her face as she once again urged thoughts of James into the back of her mind.

Mr. Haydon explained the purpose of the three literary publications that he owned as well as two small collections that were housed in the basement of the old building that had been in his family for several generations. It seemed that the business was in his blood. He led the small party out to the front of the building, past the other closed doors, and Chloe saw that the same silent young man was still sitting at his post, typing industriously. Mr. Haydon led them upstairs where rooms were filled with old copies of magazines, books and newspapers. The rooms were pleasantly dim with the pervading smell of dust and ink. A large room overlooking the street was empty save an oval table and half of a dozen chairs. In this room, he told Chloe, they had had many a meeting lasting into the late hours. On the way back downstairs he explained to Chloe that although the actual printing was done off premises, all of the proofreading and editing was done in this building. He was a thorough and very interesting host and Chloe found herself disappointed to see the end of the tour. Having worked in a small magazine for some time, she was interested to see how other offices were run. He stopped in his office where Mrs. Mainthswaite collected her umbrella and gloves, passing a trio of graying gentlemen deep in conversation. They nodded absentmindedly to the ladies and entered another of the offices. Turning to the ladies, Mr. Haydon gave his funny old fashioned bow and invited them to lunch with him. At their assent he beamed as if someone had handed him a very great treasure, and proclaimed himself 'enormously pleased'.

      Chloe followed behind as they walked out into the street. Mr. Haydon proclaimed it mild enough to walk instead of taking a taxi and it would be an opportunity for Chloe to observe even more of the great city. He suggested his club which was housed in another of the fine old buildings that the city boasted. Indeed with the sun now fully out from under its covering of clouds the air had become quite pleasant and warm. With Mr. Haydon and Mrs. Mainthswaite in the lead, Chloe walked through the sun lit streets looking at everything she could. She admired the rows of buildings, stared at the streets busy with automobile and carriage alike. It reminded her of many other walks she had taken with Fiona and James, and she experienced that sharp pang of homesickness again, but just for a moment, as they had arrived at their destination. The walk had been a brisk forty minutes and Chloe was quite happy to enter the close quiet atmosphere. Although there seemed to be a preponderance of men in the club, Chloe did see a sprinkling of richly attired women in the dining room. It shared the same elegance as the hotel where she and Mrs. Mainthswaite were staying. The warm soft lights of the room gleamed off of the dark wood paneling. Hushed voices echoed and waters in black jackets swiftly and silently went about their tasks. It quite took her breath away, having not had the fortune to visit their hotel's restaurant yet. She stared around as they were led to a square table with a crisp linen cloth. Chloe had visited the delicatessen two streets over from her little room in New York, but that was the extent of her restaurant experiences, finances being what they were. As soon as they had settled on choices for their luncheon, Chloe let her mind wander. She did not follow the conversation between Mrs. Mainthswaite and Mr. Haydon too closely as it was peppered with unknown names and past reminiscences, but she tried at least to keep one ear on it lest she be caught 'woolgathering' again. She made a mental note to remember every detail. She would sit in her room tonight keeping the curtain wide to let in the moonlight and record everything that had happened and think of her friends wishing they were there to share this all with her. How she and Fiona would enjoy a day like today. And to bring James to Mr. Haydon's wonderful office, that would be a fine time. Mr. Haydon included her in the conversation from time to time, considerately explaining sights she must see. Hyde Park was a wonderful place, and there were museums as well, if she found interest in that. Chloe eagerly nodded and asked if there were any nearby.

"Why yes, dear girl, as a matter of fact there is the National Gallery is not too far of a distance, and it's a most interesting place. Lovely building as well. You must go. "

Mrs. Mainthswaite answered for her "Yes of course, William, I will not have brought Chloe half way around the world, so to speak, to hide her in a room. " As she said this however, a smile lurked in the corner of her mouth that belied the sharpness of her tone.

The light bantering between the two old friends was amusing, and Chloe caught something from the gleam in Mr. Haydon's eyes that made her think perhaps there could be something more in time. Soon, luncheon was over and Mr. Haydon escorted the ladies back to their hotel. Mrs.

Mainthswaite planned to take some time in the afternoon to prepare some correspondence of a personal matter. It seemed that the Mainthswaite's owned some property outside of London which had been in the care of a distant relative recently deceased. While staying in London, Mrs. Mainthswaite would make preparations to sell the house as she did not plan to use it and had no younger relatives on that side of the family. Chloe was only mildly surprised at this, as she had known that Mrs. Mainthswaite still had some ties to England. Finding herself with some free time, and too excited to lie down as Mrs. Mainthswaite had suggested, she prowled restlessly around the hotel, poking into various rooms and admiring the elegant furnishings. She found herself in a small square room off the hall, almost hidden in the corner adjacent to the main lobby, where she spent a pleasurable hour investigating its shelves of books. It's dark paneling and deep burgundy leather chairs were very inviting to Chloe and reminded her of the masculine décor in Mr. Haydon's office, even down to the faint pipe tobacco scent.

The next few days sped by at a whirlwind pace, almost dizzying. Chloe was excited and exhausted at the end of each day and had no time even to feel the ache in her heart which she had grown so used to. One afternoon, they went to the museum that Mr. Haydon spoke so highly of. It was indeed remarkable. It was a grand building, big enough for a palace Chloe thought, with columns and graceful windows, set on a large square. The art captivated Chloe, and it was an ideal place for people watching. Elegant groups stood about admiring the paintings, wide brimmed hats on the women complimented their beautiful dresses. Two other days they had gone to Hyde Park, however the chilly air which had come to stay did not let them prolong their visit as much as Chloe had hoped. Following that, the rain dripped ceaselessly and the ladies found themselves indoors for the whole of the day. After several busy days this was not an unwelcome break, and Mr. Haydon, who had become a frequent visitor, accompanied the ladies to lunch. He met them in the main lobby, dripping hat in hand. After lunch, Chloe helped Mrs. Mainthswaite for a while in her room with several items of correspondence and then retired to her own room on a sudden whim to try her hand at fiction. While she did have several short stories in her battered portfolio, which lived under her bed in New York, she never felt completely comfortable with them, instead preferring to write about her own experiences and those of others. In this city, with its history and atmosphere however she felt like she could do anything.

The next day proved both exhilarating and nerve wracking. Mr. Haydon paid his customary visit and suggested that the trio hire a car and see more of the city since the sun poked its head out from behind stubborn clouds and gave them a cheery greeting. Driving around in the little car allowed Chloe the luxury of gazing out the window and resting comfortably. They drive past Buckingham Palace, grand and beautiful, and Mr. Haydon joked that by next year she would want to come back for more. As they pulled up to the hotel again, and thanked Mr. Haydon for a lovely drive, he elicited a promise from Mrs. Mainthswaite to allow him to accompany them to the theater. She graciously inclined her head, much used to events like this. Chloe however was thrown into despair, for as she had indulged in people watching, she had come to realize that her beautiful gown which had seemed so sophisticated with its slender skirt and fancy work, did not seem to be nearly fancy enough for the theater.

"But I haven't got anything that I can wear to the theater!" Chloe wailed once they reached the sanctuary of their rooms. Her distress at the lack of appropriate clothing was enough to shake her usual calm demeanor. She held up her pink dress, "this is my absolute best and it's no fancier than any of the dresses I have seen on ladies downstairs! In the afternoon!" Chloe would be sorely disappointed not to go to the theater, a once in a lifetime chance perhaps, but she had seen the looks that had passed between her employer and Mr. Haydon in recent days and how solicitous he had been towards her. She recognized the beginning of a spark between the two old friends because she felt it many times with James and didn't want to intrude upon that.

Mrs. Mainthswaite gave a delicate snort, "Fiddlesticks, you will look perfectly fine. It's a lovely dress, and much more practical than many of these young girls with their clothes half falling off. I brought my lace shawl which would make a handsome accessory. Now go put your dress on." And she shooed Chloe back into her little room to get dressed and brush her hair. Chloe did as she was told, putting on the dress, which did, she had to agree, fit her perfectly. She brushed her honey toned waves until they shone and pinned them up in a way Fiona had shown her. Returning to Mrs. Mainthswaite she studied the effect in the older lady's large vanity mirror. Mrs. Mainthswaite handed her a heavy ivory lace shawl to wrap about herself, along with matching ivory lace gloves. Chloe put them on and agreed with Mrs. Mainthswaite that the effect was "quite satisfactory". Mrs.

Mainthswaite had outdone herself for the evening. As usual she had on a dress of muted color, but its deep subtle blue set off her eyes and added color to her cheeks. The neck was fashionably wide. But for the ruched silk beneath she would have been quite cold. Her jet earrings winked in the light. Turning to Chloe she instructed the younger woman to stand still again while she surveyed Chloe minutely, and decided that there was something lacking still. After poking in her own jewel case for a few moments, she returned to where Chloe was stationed and handed her a necklace with a pale amethyst pendant. The effect was lovely indeed and

"Oh Mrs. Mainthswaite, thank you so much!" Chloe gave her a warm smile and continued to glance in the mirror surreptitiously.

"Stop gaping at yourself girl, you look neat and presentable." Mrs. Mainthswaite ushered Chloe out into the hall but not before Chloe detected the twinkle in Mrs. Mainthswaite's eyes which belied her gruff words. Thus, appropriately attired, the two ladies made their way down to the lobby to await Mr. Haydon, who picked them up in due course. The theater was everything Chloe had imagined and more. Naturally it was beautiful, glittering with chandeliers and packed with other theater goers in their very best furs and silks. Mrs. Mainthswaite entered on the arm of a very attentive Mr. Haydon who graciously included Chloe as he assisted them to their seats. His very English charm prevented him from being anything but the perfect host. The theater performance was an experience all to itself and Chloe was in awe of the musicians and the actors who graced the stage and envied their prodigious talents. The evening flew and before Chloe had much time to think, Mr. Haydon was escorting them back to the hotel for a late dinner. As they ate, he looked at her with his kindly expression. "What did you think, my dear?" Chloe didn't know quite what to say, how to sum up the exhilaration, grandeur and emotion of the evening. In the end she merely shook her head and told him she would never forget it for the rest of her life. At that the silver haired gentleman laughed and said he had hoped it had lived up to her expectations and was glad to see that was true. After dinner was over they parted ways and before her head hit the pillow she was asleep under the downy comforter dreaming of the nights entrancing performance.

The next day too was quite active though of a more mundane kind. Mrs. Mainthswaite was occupied with tasks of her own, so after their usual morning in her room and quick luncheon they parted ways. Before leaving for her appointment, Mrs. Mainthswaite informed Chloe that a cousin of hers had invited them to stay at his country house for a few days. They would take a hired car tomorrow to stay until their departure to Paris. This added to Chloe's excitement although she had fallen in love with London and would be sorry to leave.

After a busy week and a half in the city, Chloe felt quite able to navigate her way around the streets near the hotel. Since the air was not too cold and a pale watery sun peeked out from the gray sky, she bundled herself up and started out for a brisk walk to the park. She sat by a small pond watching a trio of small children being unsuccessfully shepherded by a tired looking nanny. Chloe had taken her journal with her. She wrote at times, alternately blowing on her gloveless hands for warmth or pushing them inside her pockets while feeling quite the world traveler. It was a peaceful contemplative day and she walked back through the park crunching on the fallen leaves that scattered over the broad lawns. Mrs. Mainthswaite called to her when Chloe entered her own room that she didn't feel quite like going down to the restaurant. That evening Chloe dined alone, but did not mind in the least, so many people to observe made dinner quite an interesting meal.

Chapter 19

The next day, after packing enough for a week-end stay, the two ladies bundled themselves into a car and set off for the country house of Mrs. Mainthswaite's cousin Henry Smythe. Mr. Haydon had been conspicuously absent the day before, unusual after his attentiveness, and that morning Chloe found her employer to be unusually pale and quiet. When asked if she was feeling well enough to travel, Mrs. Mainthswaite said everything was fine. Chloe wasn't sure what to make of this but fervently hoped to see the sparkle return to Mrs. Mainthswaite's otherwise severe expression.

The car jolted them for about 2 hours before turning down a broad drive lined with large trees, just tinged with the bronze and orange of autumn. Chloe thought it must be beautiful in spring. Finally after what seemed an interminable time on the private drive, the car came to a stop. Chloe peeped out of the window as Mrs. Mainthswaite muttered about the state of her nerves after the drive. The house, if it could be called that, was massive and brick. Ivy crept up one side of the house. Its many windows glinted in the bright afternoon sun, diamond pained at the top. The chauffer opened the doors for the ladies and stood waiting with their luggage. Chloe waited awkwardly, unsure of how to act in this alien atmosphere. There was a man in a black suit waiting at the door who introduced himself as Hammond, the butler. His formal manner intimidated Chloe further; however Mrs. Mainthswaite airily greeted him and stalked proudly under the archway and into the house. Chloe glanced at Hammond again, who gave a slight indication that she should precede him. The chauffer took up the rear of the strange little parade. Once inside, they were greeted by Mrs. Mainthswaite's cousin, Henry and his wife. Chloe had barely time to glance around the cavernous hall filled with light.

"Elizabeth darling, it's been too long," exclaimed Mrs. Smythe, who was a diminutive blonde lady nearing middle age. Her simple dress exuded elegance. She turned to Chloe and gave her a warm welcome. "Oh I do hope you will be comfortable, Chloe. Please do call me Mary. Henry and I hate formalities, don't we dear? Henry, I gave her the blue room, is that quite right do you think?" Without waiting for an answer from her husband, who didn't look as though the room assignments were on the top of his priorities, she swung back around and took Chloe and Mrs. Mainthswaite by the arm and steered them into the large room facing them. Henry Smythe was left to himself having given the ladies the briefest of greetings. He followed and this time was able to greet his cousin while his loquacious wife was busily chatting to Chloe.

"Did you have a comfortable journey Chloe? Elizabeth mentioned it was your first time abroad."

"Yes it is, and it was lovely. We…"

"I'm so glad you loved it, Henry and I have talked many times about a visit to our 'American cousin' but we haven't done it yet. The children, you know…" Mary trailed off then, allowing Chloe time to at least murmur a polite reply. "Oh, we should be going into lunch at any time, you can meet our son and daughter, oh, and that's right Jeremy's friend is down for the week as well." Chloe nodded, feeling quite dizzy at this onslaught of names and facts being positively thrown at her. She glanced at Mrs. Mainthswaite who was sitting in a comfortable armchair by the window facing Henry. She caught Chloe's eye and gave the barest smile, as if acknowledging how Chloe must feel. Mary had gone on to fill Chloe in on various topics of news from the nearby village, and finding that she need only a nod or smile, Chloe let her eyes wander around the room, taking in the graciously high ceilings with large bright windows. The furniture was simple and the dark wood gleamed in contrast to the light colors of the curtains and walls. There were several lovely paintings on the walls and large vases of flowers gave the room a delicate scent. It was a very comfortable homey room, despite the grandeur of the house. Presently, Hammond emerged from a door on the far side of the room and announced that luncheon was ready. Chloe was firmly guided into the dining room by her gracious hostess who had not yet stopped talking. "Oh good, here is Jeremy, and his friend Robert. Where is Maggie, Jerry?" Chloe nodded a greeting to Jeremy, and his friend Robert, sitting down in the seat indicated. She was pleased to find that it was not next to Mary, however kind she was.

A tall girl with dark hair entered and sat next to Chloe. She was so like her father that Chloe knew this must be Maggie. She had a highly sensitive face of strong features with intelligence shining from her eyes. She was about Chloe's age but at least half a head taller. Once all the introductions were made, Maggie leaned over and whispered to Chloe "Has Mother been boring you to death? She does that you know." Fortunately Chloe was saved from replying to this not altogether tactful statement by Jeremy Smythe, who objected loudly to something his father was telling him. The rest of the luncheon passed pleasantly. Chloe chatted with Maggie for the most part, joined from time to time by Robert, who evidently was quite familiar with the family. Chloe caught something of a strong current between Maggie and Robert. The young man kept his eyes fixed on her mobile face throughout the luncheon and whenever Maggie happened to meet his eyes, her face reddened and she looked away hurriedly. Knowing something of the same feeling with James, Chloe hid her amused smile and kept her attention on the conversation. As the lunch ended, Mary suggested that Maggie take Chloe for a walk around the grounds.

"Yes, Chloe, that would be a good idea. Go enjoy yourself." Mrs. Mainthswaite put in. Maggie nodded as well.

Chloe duly followed Maggie out the front door along the curving path that led to the side of the broad lawn, and down the gentle slope toward a meandering creek. The sun was warm and the air had a pleasant autumn smell. The two girls spend a pleasant afternoon on the grounds and then went into the village, a mile up the road. It was picturesque and old fashioned, exactly as Chloe would have imagined an English village to be. Maggie gave Chloe a brief history of the town and also included any juicy bits of gossip, which, although unfamiliar with the village, she found quite entertaining. Chloe in turn told Maggie about her home, and how she had moved from Stuflen to New York. Maggie expressed admiration and amazement for Chloe's initiative and independence and asked many questions about her life in New York. Soon it was time to return to the house and the girls trudged back up the gentle slope until they could see the house in the distant, standing solid and square with its many chimneys.

The three older family members were sitting in the drawing room still, immersed in discussion. Jeremy and his friend were nowhere to be seen. Maggie muttered to Chloe that they had most probably taken the horses out for a ride.

"Hello ladies" boomed Henry jovially, standing to include Chloe and Maggie. "Did you have a nice walk?" His broad face was quite weather beaten but genial and warm. It was obvious that he and his daughter were very close.

Before either could utter a word however his wife began her own interrogation "My goodness you were out for a while weren't you? I was beginning to wonder. Where did you take her, Maggie? Wasn't the village quaint, Chloe?" Mary turned without waiting for an answer and began speaking to Mrs. Mainthswaite, who looked as if she could use a bit of quiet.

Maggie shot Chloe a look of amusement. "Mother, please don't monopolize Cousin Elizabeth so, I should think it's time for us to show our guests to their rooms. I'm sure they need to refresh." Whirling toward the door in her customary energetic manner, Maggie pulled the bell and instructed an attractive maid to show Chloe and Mrs. Mainthswaite to their rooms. As they followed her, Chloe flashed Maggie a grateful look and was rewarded by an impish smile.

The maid led them up the wide staircase which opened on a long hall. She opened one of the doors and ushered Mrs. Mainthswaite in showing her where her case had been placed.

"Thank you…?"

"Lily, Ma'am"

"Thank you Lily, this is most acceptable. Chloe, I believe I shall rest for a bit. Lily, would you be so kind as to show Chloe to her room? "

Lily nodded "Yes Ma'am. Miss Chloe will be staying 3 doors down, on the left." With that she turned smartly, her starched uniform rustling, and led the way before Chloe could so much as glance in Mrs. Mainthswaite's room. She led the way down the hall and opened the door into a large bright room. It was indeed blue Chloe noted; the wall color matched the bed linens to perfection. The furniture was simple yet elegant. A wide fireplace graced one wall, with small desk and chair facing the window. It looked most inviting, and as soon as Chloe had thanked Lily, the maid, she closed the door and threw herself across the bed, sinking into the comfortable mattress. She must have dozed off for a bit, for when she opened her eyes to a tapping on the door, the sun was sinking below the tree line, dimming the bedroom. Maggie stood in the doorway, carrying what appeared to be a large bulky box in her arms.

"Oh. Am I bothering you?" Maggie looked uncertainly at Chloe whose hair was undoubtedly rumpled from the bed.

"Not at all, I must have drifted off. Come in Maggie."

Maggie leapt into the room in a manner which Chloe was beginning to realize was characteristic of her. "Oh, here, Chloe. I've come bearing gifts. Well, one, that is. From cousin Elizabeth." Maggie beamed and plopped the oblong box on Chloe's bed.

Chloe, still slightly foggy from her brief nap, shook her head to clear the cobwebs. "I'm sorry Maggie, what is this?"

"It's from my cousin. She asked me to bring it to you. Oh do open it up, let's see what you have." Not waiting for an answer, Maggie slipped the brown string off of the box and lifted the cover to reveal a mound of reddish wool. Maggie lifted it up to Chloe. It was a skirt, underneath, still nestled in the box was a blouse.

"Oh," breathed Chloe. "It's just beautiful!" She picked up the blouse, which was patterned delicately in reddish and rust hues. The girls, each holding a garment, giggled in unison. "Why ever did Mrs. Mainthswaite get this for me? And when?"

"That, I'm afraid is going to have to wait. I am sure she will tell you all about it at dinner. In the meantime let's get you into this; I am simply dying to see it on you." With a push she motioned Chloe toward the tall screen in the corner of her room and handed over the skirt. Chloe quickly acquiesced, being eager to see the outfit herself. She came out from behind the screen and turned to Maggie. What do you think?"

"It's gorgeous. Fits superbly too. Come look at yourself in my room."

Chloe followed Mary down the hall into another room, larger and with more personality naturally. Maggie had a few comfortable chairs and a table along one wall, next to the fireplace, and on another was her dressing table and a full length mirror which Chloe went to and looked at herself critically. She couldn't deny that it looked good, and even though the color was bolder than she herself would have chosen, it brought out the honey tints in her hair and gave her a little more color in her pale face. She turned around to see that Maggie had slumped despondently into one of the armchairs by the fireplace. Chloe came over and sat facing her. "Maggie, what's the matter? "

"Oh, it's Robert."

Chloe looked at her questioningly, waiting for her to elaborate. She had seen the glances and knew there must be something behind Maggie's sudden depression. "Well, you see, tonight we're having another guest come, it's a friend of my father, well a younger friend, and he's terribly wealthy.

Nothing has been made official of course, but, well, I know Mother and Father are hoping we will marry. I don't doubt he would want it as well." Maggie looked scornfully at the ground, as if the gentleman in question was no better than a snail. "I don't want to marry him at all, I'd much rather marry Robert. But he's not very well off. That doesn't matter in the slightest to me. Oh I know I am used to things being nicely done and having to never clean or cook, but I wouldn't mind, not at all."

Chloe was a bit taken aback at this rush of confidences, but she liked Maggie immensely and hoped that she would not end up marrying someone she did not want to. It was obvious that Maggie was in despair about the situation. "Maggie, you can't do something just to please your parents. If you're completely certain, then you must tell them. Have you and Robert an agreement? Or has he made it know what his feelings are? I must tell you it looked as if he feels the same, judging by what I saw at lunch."

"Oh yes, we have spoken about it at great length and he knows how my parents feel, at any rate not about him, but about Ian, he is the friend of my father's. " Maggie paused with a sidelong glance at Chloe. "You could tell at lunch?"

"Yes I could tell. But then he was sitting directly across from me. "

Maggie leaned back "Oh dear, I suppose it is pretty obvious. From the moment Jerry brought him home for a weekend I suppose actually. Robert is so intelligent; he is a doctor you know. Well he is going to be starting his own practice very soon. I think it's a wonderful profession, but Mother and Father, well; they have old fashioned views of course. Oh, it's wonderful to have someone to talk to about all this. Not having any sisters, or any cousins to speak of really. Ian is quite good looking, so of course all of my friends don't understand why I don't want to marry him immediately." She sighed, toying with the edge of her sleeve. "So, do you think I have a hope?"

"Of course, Maggie. Your parents aren't going to be too disappointed. I'm sure they would much rather have a happy daughter than a rich miserable one. They seem very kind."

"Yes they are of course, I suppose your right. I just have to time it right. I know Ian is coming here with the intention of proposing. I didn't want to make a scene and I certainly didn't expect Jerry to bring Robert down yesterday."

Maggie sighed deeply. "Chloe, my parents are so hopeful that I will marry well. Despite all our appearances, we aren't very well off. Half of this house is not even used and the land is getting quite difficult to keep up. Jerry is very smart but he isn't interested in the country life. I'm afraid it's all on me to keep this old place going. A country doctor with no inheritance would certainly not be able to satisfy their requirements."

"Maggie," Chloe soothed. "I've hardly been here a day, yet I just can't seem to see how your parent's would be that callous not to consider your happiness."

"No, perhaps you have a point there. I am afraid I overreact sometimes. I still dread tonight."

"Well, at least you have some different guests' this evening. Perhaps that will take the tension away somewhat."

Maggie stood then. "You're so calming Chloe; I do believe I can survive tonight after all, although I dread it still. Well we should start dressing for dinner. She looked out the window; the darkening sky met the line of trees in the distance. Down below shone the pinpoints of headlights approaching. Maggie saw them and shuddered. "Here comes Ian, let the fun begin." She grinned. "I'll send Lily in to do your hair. She does it so well."

"Thank you so much Maggie. Oh, I meant to ask, what should I wear to dinner? I haven't brought much naturally."

"Hmm, what do you have?" Maggie asked and as Chloe obediently opened her small bag and brought out the pink dress and a spare skirt and blouse, Maggie advised her to wear the pink dress. "That's simply beautiful Chloe, it will do perfectly." She ushered Chloe back to her own room to see to her own toilet, still noticeably perturbed about the arrival of her unwanted suitor.

Chloe quickly changed into her pink dress, still marveling at the detail and perfect fit, and carefully hung her new outfit in the wardrobe. She sat at the dressing table and surveyed her appearance. A few moments later the maid tapped lightly and inquired about the state of Chloe's hair. Although she was quite unused to it, Chloe enjoyed the experience of having her hair done, and thought the style looked lovely.

She ran lightly down the stairs to the drawing room, meeting Mrs. Mainthswaite on the landing and thanking her profusely for her overly generous gift.

"I'm glad you like it Chloe. It seemed to be appropriate, and I thought the color would suit you. With our impending trip to Paris, it would be good to have an additional outfit, especially as it gets a bit chillier." Mrs. Mainthswaite maintained her usual brusque exterior but her eyes twinkled deceptively. The two ladies waited in the drawing room for the other members of the party.

In due course, the rest of the family and Robert joined them. The ill awaited Ian was announced. He was indeed a good looking man; Chloe saw that Maggie had not been remiss in her observations. Not quite as tall as Robert and Jerry, he had thick fair hair and blue eyes which looked at everyone good naturedly under fair brows. He was perhaps 10 years older than Maggie. Although Robert was not so conventionally handsome, he had more individuality and strength of character in his expression than Ian. Introductions were made for the newcomers benefit and dinner was served. Chloe saw that both Maggie and her mother had beautiful gowns on in pale blue and cream respectively, both generously endowed with lace. Mrs. Mainthswaite had her pale gold dress, which was quite suitable for any occasion.

The dinner proceeded without incident, although Chloe could see that the atmosphere was tingling with barely suppressed tension. The older members of the family chatted nonchalantly. Maggie kept her eyes on her plate for most of the dinner, responding conversationally to remarks from Ian as noncommittally as possible. Chloe sat next to Jerry, and sought to keep a conversation going but found it difficult in the face of Robert's thunderous looks. Blissfully unaware of the tension, Ian included each person in turn in his conversation. Despite Maggie's feelings, Chloe found him to be an interesting person although she did not quite hold with his ideals.

Thankfully dinner was finally over, but as the ladies filed into the drawing room again as was custom, Ian caught Maggie by the arm and quietly inquired if they could find a private place to converse. Avoiding Robert's troubled expression; Maggie stared at Chloe and silently beseeched her to do something.

"Oh, er, Maggie, You were going to show me the, um, conservatory after dinner?" Chloe weakly tried to intervene, but Ian smoothly interrupted and led an unwilling Maggie away.

Chloe waited tensely in the drawing room for her to return, and felt as if the clock must have stopped altogether. Finally after what seemed an age, Maggie returned pale faced. Her eyes burned brightly with determination. Motioning Chloe over, she whispered that she would tell her later, and went to answer her mother's repeated questions. Before five minutes had passed, however, Ian entered, giving a stiff apology that he must return to London. Bowing briefly to the ladies, his eyes lingering on Maggie, he left.

"Well, do you know what that was about Margaret?" Her mother turned on her, and Chloe could only imagine that from the tone of her voice, that she was not happy.

Feeling a tug on her sleeve, Chloe turned to Mrs. Mainthswaite who was motioning her toward the door. The two left Maggie and her mother in private, Mrs. Mainthswaite remarking on the shortsightedness of trying to run one's daughter's life for her. With that observation, the two parted company and sought the comfort of their rooms. Chloe took advantage of the silence, and, settling at the dainty desk under the window which looked out open a clear starry night, brought out her journal. She wrote for some time, listening to the crackling of the small fire which had been laid while she was at dinner. She wrote as descriptively as possible, knowing full well how much Fiona would love to hear about such a grand house as this. She wrote about the romance that she had unknowingly become involved in and the personalities in the house. Then on impulse, probably brought on by observing Maggie's problems, she pulled a blank sheet out of the back of her journal and scrawled a short but heartfelt letter to James. She was sure Maggie would post it for her. Looking out at the darkness, watching the same sliver of moon which looked down on James, she felt closer to him then she had in several weeks. She felt at peace with her emotions but missed him terribly. Letting herself think about him hurt but it was worthwhile. She slipped into her bed and into a dreamless sleep. That is until an insistent knocking at her door pulled her into wakefulness. The room was dark. She surmised she had not been asleep for very long. Upon her answer the door swung open to admit Maggie, in her dressing gown, hair hanging down her back in a long braid. Chloe ushered her in and as Maggie perched on the end of the bed with her chin on her knees, Chloe was struck by how much younger she looked without her fancy trimmings and perfect hair.

"What happened tonight?" Chloe asked simply.

"It went horribly" Maggie wailed, voice muffled in her night gown. "He… he asked me and then I simply stood there. I didn't know what to do. He almost took that as an acceptance, and then I said no. I should have been so much more polite about it but I was just frozen. Oh, he was angry and icy. He said he didn't understand my decision but that it wasn't going to affect his friendship with my father. Oh, he acted as if I should thank him for being such friends with Father." She sighed and stretched then, lying limply across the bottom of the bed. I have been up with Mother and Father, both of them arguing at me and about me. I didn't even see Robert; he made himself scarce as soon as Ian left. I don't know what I should do. I want to talk to him. I don't want him to think I have accepted Ian. What should I do Chloe?"

Chloe tried to sooth the agitated girl, feeling as if it were her own sister she was comforting. "I think you need to speak to Robert as soon as possible. If he feels that you are going to marry Ian he will probably want to leave as soon as possible. Don't wait on your feelings Maggie."

"Your right Chloe, oh you have made me feel better again today. Of course he knows my feelings, but family obligations can be so strong. I don't know what I'll do when you leave. I'll talk to him right away, well first thing in the morning. You will come with me? Please? May I come get you? I just don't want him to be angry."

"He is not going to go away without talking to you. But yes, I'll come with you although I don't know why you need me."

"If you had grown up in a house like this you would realize how much the servants would talk about he and I meeting privately early in the morning. It's like having a second set of parents sometimes." Maggie grinned to show Chloe that she was certainly not to be envied to have grown up in a rather well off family with many servants.

Chloe agreed to accompany Maggie, and breathed a sigh of relief when the younger girl returned to her own room. "What a nest of drama I seem to have landed myself in." Chloe murmured to herself. She heartily hoped that Maggie was able to speak with Robert as she wished, and that this whole misunderstood situation would work itself out in short order. Barely had she closed her eyes, did Chloe hear a knocking at her door. It seemed that morning had come although Chloe didn't even remember slipping into sleep. Maggie opened the door slightly and peeped in, her pale cheeks accentuated the strain showing in her eyes, although she had taken care to dress attractively in a wool skirt which reached to her ankles and a heavy blouse and wool fitted jacket. "One moment Maggie." Chloe hastened to dress in her old blue skirt, since she surmised that she would be able to return to bed as soon as the young couple had relinquished her.

Soon they slipped quietly down to the other end of the house in the gloom of early morning, to tap at Robert's door. All was quiet except for the ticking of a clock somewhere near, and the faint clanking and shuffling of the fires being lit downstairs. After a few minutes they heard a mumbled expletive and creaking of floorboards. Robert opened his door, having hastily thrown on a dressing gown. His hair was disheveled and he was rubbing the sleep out of his eyes. As he became aware of his company, his face showed the appropriate astonishment at being awoken at such an hour by Maggie. He motioned them to wait, and without a word slipped back into his room. Barely a minute later, he reappeared, fully if carelessly dressed and followed them out into the alcove at the front of the house, away from the other bedrooms.

"Maggie? Chloe? What are you doing at this hour? Is anything the matter?"

Maggie looked at Chloe, who took charge of the situation. "Robert, Maggie is very, er eager to speak with you…regarding last night. She asked me to accompany her at this early hour lest you feel the need to leave earlier than anticipated." Maggie nodded her agreement. "Maggie, perhaps you should take Robert downstairs into the drawing room."

"Yes, I'm sure that's a good idea. I believe the fire is already made up in there. We could go in there and it wouldn't be improper at all."

"Yes, Maggie and Robert, why don't you do that."

"You are coming aren't you?" Maggie's eyes pleaded with her and Chloe, despite her interrupted night, agreed.

The trio headed downstairs, walking past a surprised Hammond and made for the drawing room, its fire burning brightly and casting away the chill. An awkward silence stretched, until Chloe stood, and resolutely walked over to the far end of the room on the pretense of studying the three peaceful landscapes on the wall. Luckily there were two books on one of the round tables. They were not of a very interesting topic to Chloe but ideal to leaf through and give Maggie and Robert a longer period of privacy. Out of the corner of her eye she saw Maggie speaking earnestly, her voice too low to be heard. Presently, however the two stood, heads inclined toward each other, and Chloe surmised the conversation had gone well. The door to the hall opened and the ever proper Hammond stood there. Addressing Maggie he said "I took the liberty of laying some breakfast and tea in the dining room, Miss Margaret, seeing that you had risen." Maggie thanked him prettily and suggested they adjourn to the dining room. Seeing this as her opportunity, Chloe quickly excused herself and encouraged the other two to enjoy the early meal. Maggie flashed her a look of gratitude and happiness and they parted ways, Chloe to her room to throw herself back into bed, and wonder how well her new friend had fared. By the look of it, Maggie had fared very well indeed.

Later that morning, when Chloe had woken for the second time feeling quite refreshed, she changed into her new skirt and blouse and made her way downstairs to the dining room where a full breakfast was laid out. The only two occupants were Mrs. Mainthswaite and Jerry, who was on the point of leaving but stopped for a few polite words. Chloe took a seat opposite Mrs. Mainthswaite at the large table, helping herself to toast and bacon. The sunlight streamed in through the lace curtains covering the broad windows making lace patterns across the floor. When asked if she had a refreshing night sleep, Chloe looked at her employer for a moment, considering the night and replied noncommittally that it had not been as refreshing as she had hoped. The two discussed their plans to return to London later that afternoon and then lapsed into a comfortable silence while Mrs. Mainthswaite perused the newspaper abandoned by Jerry.

Presently Henry Smythe entered the room, suitably dressed in country tweeds and looking as if he had been for a long walk about the property. He graciously invited Chloe to come look at his prizes in the conservatory as he called them. Chloe agreed, wondering if he too had a fitful night as evidenced by his somber cast, however jovial he tried to appear.

He led the way toward the back of the house, making a right off of the main hall into an area where Chloe had not been. There the two entered a smallish room, obviously an addition on the original structure. It was a bright space, full of light from the many windows and glassed ceiling and covered in vines and flowers. Henry, always an enthusiastic gardener, extolled the virtues of this and that plant, leaving Chloe to nod and admire the glossy leaves and bright colors. She noticed however that for all of his enthusiasm he appeared to be slightly distracted. When she ventured to inquire if he was quite all right, he just smiled sadly and said that everything was fine. The two spent a pleasant hour among the flowers and returned to the main part of the house where Maggie and Robert were divesting themselves of outer garments. At her questioning glance, Maggie gave Chloe a grimace and a discreet thumbs-up, which Chloe took to mean that she had spoken to her mother and had received a very grudging approval. Although longing to know more, Chloe dutifully followed her host outside to view the horses and stables. Although Maggie had shown her the outer building briefly the day before, Chloe listened patiently to Henry until such time as they could return to the house. At least it was a fair day, breezy and slightly overcast, but not unduly chilly, Chloe reflected. After her very thorough tour, Chloe went in search of her employer to find out what time they would be leaving that afternoon and to pack up her belongings.

Chloe finished putting her dress and extra skirt away when Maggie appeared at the door, smiling broadly despite the shadows of sleeplessness under her eyes. "Well it's all been settled. More or less. Although my parents are not ecstatic of course, but we knew they wouldn't be."

"Good for you Maggie! I'm proud of you for standing up to your parents. I can imagine it wasn't easy."

Maggie laughed shortly. "No it certainly wasn't. They hemmed and hawed and argued all of Ian's positive points. Which of course there are many, I'm not disputing that." She sighed. "Of course it would have been easier to fall in love with him, and then everyone would have been happy. But it doesn't happen that way does it?"

'No." Chloe thought of James and their tentative feelings and her stubbornness. "No, it never happens the way you had planned."

"Ah well. Robert and I are blissfully happy at least, and even though it will be an awfully long engagement, until he has his own practice and house, I couldn't ask for more." Maggie linked Chloe's arm through her own. "Let's go down to lunch, it should be any minute, come see the drama." Together they ran lightly down the stairs to lunch and spent the remainder of the visit secreted in Maggie's old nursery on the third floor, sharing confidences and many laughs.

That afternoon the family gathered to bid their cousin and new friend goodbye.

Maggie gave Chloe a fierce hard hug and whispered "I could never have stood up to my parents if you were not here. Thank you. Thank you for all of your good advice. I certainly hope that one day I can travel to the States and visit you." After many more hugs and well wishes, Chloe and Mrs. Mainthswaite, and their baggage returned to

London. Chloe felt as if she was returning home, so familiar was the grand hotel.

The very next day of course Chloe and Mrs. Mainthswaite would embark upon their third adventure and cross the Channel into France. After packing what they would need for the trip, the two ladies supped lightly and enjoyed a pleasant hour in the lounge where crackling fires at either end of the room created a cheery atmosphere. Attempting to turn in early however proved a difficult task for Chloe, despite her previous night's adventures. She had so many thoughts whirling through her mind that sleep seemed impossible. In the end, after what seemed like an eternity, but was probably closer to a half hour, she sat up with a sigh and decided to stop trying. She drew back the heavy curtains so that the full moon shone brightly on her and opened her journal which had become her dearest friend and confidant. Once she emptied her cluttered mind onto the paper, all the thoughts and experiences of the last few days, organizing the thoughts into cohesive passages, she knew that it may be easier to sleep.

The moon watched her as she filled page after page, looking down on her like a benevolent spirit. She created pictures of English village life with her words and wrote about the family with whom she felt a distinct connection. Many times however, she found that it was not all of these exciting and new experiences that her thoughts revolved around but of New York and Fiona and most specifically James. In these quiet times, when her mind was left to its own devices without the demands of sightseeing and conversation, she missed him more than ever. She thought about that brief exhilarating moment right before leaving when she felt his arms around her so safe and warm. The thought of his lips on hers brought up a blush every time she thought of it. She wondered if his thoughts were as intense and frightening and filled with longing, wondered if he stayed up nights looking at the same moon thinking of her and missing her. She thought of his piercing blue eyes, bluer than any ocean and how those eyes had been able to look deep into her soul from the moment they met.

Light crept underneath her eyelids and Chloe reluctantly woke to early morning and glittering rain on the window. Once she had shaken the sleep from her head Chloe realized she had fallen asleep in a sitting position, with her journal still laying open on her lap. Groaning slightly at her stiff neck and shoulders, she commenced to ring for breakfast and to prepare for the day's journey.

Chapter 20

The trip to France was uneventful although much less comfortable than their previous voyage had been. The night had taken its toll on Chloe and she felt as tired and wan as Mrs. Mainthswaite looked. The excitement which had buoyed Chloe for the last few days, making her eyes sparkle in the most becoming way, had, for the moment left. Chloe was content to sit quietly listening to the sound of the gulls and ship, bundled in her thick coat and a shawl against the cold air. Her employer was as grim as Chloe had ever seen, as she sat ramrod straight against the wooden seat. Chloe could only surmise that with the weekend behind them, her concerns regarding Mr. Haydon had returned. Chloe had half hoped that he would present himself this morning, however there was no sign of him. Their trip to Paris had come at a perfect time it seemed.

What seemed like forever ended, when finally the angry water ceased to rock the boat to and fro and produce unpleasant sensations among its passengers. Preparing for the strong winds to buffet them, for it was beginning to feel like winter had come already, they departed without ceremony and found their hired car as quickly as possible. The ride resembled the last one, Chloe tried her best to keep her eyes open, but due to the lack of sleep last night, it was an impossible task. Once the car had stopped and emptied its subdued passengers, Chloe was able to find one last piece of energy and appreciate the ornate décor and sparkling chandeliers of the fancy French hotel. The carpets were as thick and as luxuriant as those in London, but here the curtained windows and thick wall hangings glowed with rich color, as if the sun shone even late into the evening in this renowned old city. Sleep came immediately to the two ladies in their respective rooms. Morning would be soon enough to examine and appreciate each detail of the hotel and of the city, but for now, soft down beds and warm blankets were all they needed.

It seemed as though it was only minutes later that bright cold sunlight filtered through the windows which Chloe had not had the energy to cover. It filled the room with a golden light that was misleading as the room itself was filled with chilly air. A knock from the communicating door told her that Mrs. Mainthswaite was awake and fully dressed. Upon seeing her employer, Chloe realized she had overslept long after her time. She jumped up with a start, wrapping a blanket about her to keep some of the warmth from escaping.

"There is no need to rush Chloe, I had an early appointment to keep and did not require your services. As we do have several days to spend, it's best to sleep when you can. Once you are dressed, please join me in my room. I have some correspondence to go over and I had a fresh pot of coffee and pastries brought up. Perhaps once that is over you might like to take in some sights if that is satisfactory?" Her eyes twinkled as she said this, for she knew how much Chloe had longed to see Paris.

Chloe felt the excitement course through her body as she looked ahead to the day. "Yes, of course Mrs. Mainthswaite. I will get dressed immediately and hasten to assist you in any way." She turned toward her small bag, which she had tossed in a corner the night before. Mrs. Mainthswaite hid a smile as she started to close the door. "Mrs. Mainthswaite?" Chloe stood over her bag, skirt in one hand and blouse and sweater in another.

"Yes?"

"Are we really going to see the whole city?"

"As much as time allows. If the weather stays mild enough we shall take a walk through some of the surrounding streets"

A smile lit Chloe's face as she stayed lost in thought for some moments until a cough and a sarcastic "Really, girl, you would think we were going to the moon." from her employer directed Chloe back towards reality. She flashed a sheepish grin at Mrs. Mainthswaite and hurried to get dressed and present herself for whatever tasks were required of her. She dressed in her new skirt and blouse, grateful for the cream colored wool sweater that Maggie had pressed her to take. It was two years old and although it looked quite new, it had gotten shrunken from washing. Chloe was glad of the new outfit in Paris, for it seemed like it should be a very fashionable city. She would still look quite provincial, but at least had some new style. She smoothed her hair back into a simple tortoiseshell clasp she had bought, and hurried to Mrs. Mainthswaite's room. Ignoring the delectable smells wafting from a silver tray on the ornate table by the door, she gathered a notebook and pencil, preparing to forge ahead with the day. After the two worked together for some time, dealing with various correspondences from Mrs. Mainthswaite's large collection of acquaintances on this side of the Atlantic Ocean, Chloe's stomach began to rumble in earnest and she found herself no longer able to keep her mind on her work.

"Oh really, Chloe do get a pasty and some coffee. There's no need to abstain on my behalf. I ate ages ago." Mrs. Mainthswaite's voice was stern but the corner of her mouth twitched with amusement at Chloe's gastric gaffe.

"I'm sorry Mrs. Mainthswaite. I'll skip the coffee, but the pasty looks delicious." Good was an understatement, she found as she piled the flaky buttery pastries high on her plate, along with some fruit.

"It is quite good; however I do think Mrs. Kingston might teach them a trick or two." Chloe privately thought that nothing could be quite as wonderful as this, but she agreed, for Mrs. Kingston was indeed an outstanding cook, as well as a dear friend.

The ladies continued working until close to noon, when they donned coats. Chloe borrowed a scarf to cover her head, and she found it to be very attractive indeed as more sensible than a hat which would be blown off without the sharp hat pin. The sun shone brightly in the blue sky, casting sharp shadows on the pavement. Although it truly felt like fall now, the passing ladies had such fashionable attire that Chloe would have felt quite dowdy, had she not been overcome with excitement and anticipation at seeing such a center of art and intellect as this. First the two decided to sample some of the delicious smells emanating from the carts that were clustered around the area. Chloe found that nothing could compare to the bowl of creamy soup and crusty bread that she ate while leaning against a low wall bordering a park like space, something that she never thought to do with the ever proper Mrs. Mainthswaite. It seemed that a large number of couples were doing the same as Chloe and Mrs. Mainthswaite, and they were in good company as they strolled about the city. Finally Chloe was able to see the Eiffel tower with her own eyes. Always she had stood in awe of this architectural wonder. It was no less impressive in person. Its stark iron frame reaching up to divide the great blue sky in two. This being the highlight of the day for Chloe, she walked the chilly sunny streets with Mrs. Mainthswaite and gazed in awe in every direction, but try as she might, most of the day was a fog. They ate dinner in the hotel dining room that night, feasting on delicious stew with a delicate sauce. It was both light and filling. That night, Chloe snuggled deep into the down bed after her nightly entry in her journal and thought of the beautiful day. As the moon peeked into her room, a sharp sliver in the hard frosty night, she did spare a drowsy thought for her own home so far away and for the company that waited for her with longing, but as her eyelids closed the thoughts soon dissipated into dreams.

    The next day was filled with both pleasure and business as Chloe accompanied Mrs. Mainthswaite to several appointments and meetings, keeping herself invisible for the most part, just a sensibly dressed companion to assist Mrs. Mainthswaite. For all of Chloe's experience and newfound knowledge of the world, she was as shy as a schoolgirl in the company of such learned acquaintances. In the afternoon Chloe took a walk by herself, keeping an eye on her surroundings so she would not become lost. She enjoyed this immensely as people watching had always been a passion of hers. It seemed that Paris was the perfect place for people watching. She saw a myriad of people, fashionable ladies in skirts so narrow as to constrict their walking, with furs trailing off of their shoulders, and the not so fashionable, like the elderly man in patched trousers and colorful knotted scarf trying to catch a few coins as he strummed his guitar. She realized that for all the silks and furs and fine feathers the ladies and gentleman who graced the streets were very like those in New York. Watching carts and peddlers pulling their wares reinforced the feeling of being at home, except that she understood nothing of the French language. Unfortunate as it was, it was not thought to be a useful skill in the farming town where she grew up. The most she could manage was to read a few lines of Latin.

The next day was filled with similar occupations, Chloe and Mrs. Mainthswaite leaving some extra time to stroll through the museum which boasted so many works of art. The building was gracious and immense. Apparently, Mrs. Mainthswaite informed Chloe, the Louvre had been a palace, long ago. Chloe enjoyed all of the wonderful paintings, especially those more modern ones with bright colors and bold strokes. They seemed to satisfy an inner wildness that she did not show to the public. She knew Fiona would feel the same, if she were here. Mrs. Mainthswaite preferred the sedate landscapes and realistic portraits. Chloe found herself lingering more and more, feeding her eyes, knowing that she would not be able to see these again. She closed her eyes to memorize them, imagining herself describing them to Fiona and James, writing pages and pages to her sister and brothers. That night Chloe was steeped in colorful memories of the wonderful paintings she had seen, even if they had not been able to cover the whole of the museum. She could almost see the swirls of reds and violets in her journal pages.

Before she knew it, Chloe realized it was the morning of their last day in Paris. She felt some regret at this, but also anticipated the return to London. The entire trip was more wonderful than she could have imagined, yet as each day passed, she knew it was one day less to her return to New York, and whatever lay ahead. She had another reason for looking forward to their return to London. Mrs. Mainthswaite seemed to have returned to her usual acerbic manner. The pale smudges and despondent attitude was gone. Late that morning as Chloe was working on some correspondence of Mrs. Mainthswaite's, and packing it in its leather bound folder, as they would need it until the return to New York, her employer stepped through the door with a resolute look on her face. Chloe looked up, expecting some instructions of some kind.

"Chloe, I have procured tickets to the opera for tonight as it is our last evening here. An acquaintance of myself and Edward's lives in Paris and has generously included us in her group. The opera will be in Italian, but I do think you will appreciate the music. It is always important to experience as much as possible when one is able." The older woman had turned her back to Chloe as she was speaking so did not see what effect she had. Chloe was stunned and excited. She thanked Mrs. Mainthswaite profusely, which of course was shrugged off in the most delicate way. She quickly finished packing up the correspondence and came to sit down beside Mrs. Mainthswaite. The relationship between the women had become less professional and more relaxed. Especially in Paris. Chloe felt as she was fulfilling more of a companion role than a secretary, which she didn't mind in the slightest. She was gaining so much experience and felt truly like a world traveler.

"What time are we to go?" Chloe was imagining that they would not have much time in the afternoon.

"I believe we should be preparing ourselves in late afternoon. The opera will not begin until later, of course. In addition, I had the great surprise to 'bump' into one of your friends from the ship and she insisted on us meeting here for dinner when she heard of our theater plans." Mrs. Mainthswaite tried to hide her amusement. Chloe could tell from her tone that it must be her friend Hyacinth Wiggenham that Mrs. Mainthswaite had seen.

"Really? Did you see Hyacinth? What is she doing here? How long is she here for? I did not know she would be in Paris."

"I doubt she did either, my dear. I practically ran into her on the corner near our hotel. She mentioned she had come on a 'spur of the moment' decision because her daughter wanted some ridiculously styled dress for a ball. As for how long she is here, I did not find that out either. You may ask her tonight. She is meeting us in the lobby at 6:30. We can dine here." The look Mrs. Mainthswaite gave Chloe when she mentioned Hyacinth's daughter made Chloe impatient to hear about this supposedly ridiculous dress.

"I can hardly believe it. What a pleasure it will to be able to meet with Hyacinth again when I did not think to see her for quite a long time." Mrs. Mainthswaite smiled indulgently and gave a sarcastic snort to show her own opinion. She waved Chloe off, telling her to go enjoy the afternoon as it was the last day of their little Parisian adventure. Chloe decided to walk in the afternoon sunshine and soak in more sights. She came upon the same little man with his patched trousers and his beautiful guitar. After watching him for some time, she plucked up her courage to speak with him, on the off chance that he spoke English. As luck would have it, the talented gentleman spoke a very small bit of English and between his halting words and many gestures, Chloe was able to find out that his name was Philippe and he had been a bricklayer, working on many buildings around the great city. After being told that he was now too old to work, he decided to hone his first boyhood love, music. He supplemented his small pittance from passersby, but his satisfaction came from providing the beautiful music for all to hear. Chloe loved the story and rushed back to the hotel to write it all down before she could forget. She was so pleased with her efforts that she showed Mrs. Mainthswaite who exhibited admiration for the manuscript, who asked if she might keep it for a few days so that she could read it more thoroughly. After agreeing to this, Chloe returned to her quarters to begin preparations for dinner, as the hour was nearing late afternoon. Chloe could hardly contain her excitement at the prospect of seeing Hyacinth once again. As opposite as the two ladies had appeared on the surface, they found that they shared many of the same interests, including a great interest in human nature.

Chloe and Mrs. Mainthswaite took care to dress warmly, for however warm the sun shone during the day, it was autumn and the nights were quite cold. The only dress fancy enough for the opera was the pink; however this was not very warm, so Chloe layered. She had only her coat, but wore her sweater as well which she could take off in the theater. She did not attempt to emulate any of the latest fashion trends, especially when they were so far removed from her experience. Fiona had made her new dress very well and its beautiful detail provided quite enough fashion for Chloe. After dressing, Chloe descended to the lobby ahead of Mrs. Mainthswaite, to wait for her friend. Mrs. Mainthswaite had elected to remain in her room slightly longer to allow Chloe more of a change to catch up on Hyacinth's affairs and also because Hyacinth was not the ideal dinner companion in Mrs. Mainthswaite's eyes.

By the time Chloe entered the lobby, the sky was beginning to darken and she could feel the draft of cold air whenever the ornate front door was opened. She settled herself to wait for Hyacinth in one of the cream colored armchairs facing the entrance. A particularly large bundle of furs came in with a blast of chilly air not 10 minutes later and Hyacinth's face emerged from the depths of a widely brimmed hat. Chloe jumped up to greet her friend enthusiastically as Hyacinth shed what must have been twenty pounds of wraps, mufflers and a fur trimmed wool coat.

Finally, the plump matronly woman emerged to be hugged and greeted affectionately. She was wearing an unexpectedly tidy suit, in heather colored wool, but true to form, Hyacinths hat was askew and her hair was escaping from the tidy knot she wore at the back of her head. The large fire roared cheerily in the grate at one end of the lobby. The ladies moved nearer so that Hyacinth could warm her hands.

"Oh my dear, what a surprise I got when I saw Elizabeth Mainthswaite. You could have bowled me over with a feather!" Her loud tones caused a few of the other patrons to glance over disapprovingly, but only for a minute. "I didn't figure on coming over here, I can tell you." She lowered her voice in confidence. "My daughter is having a fancy ball for her engagement and wanted a particular style of dress. Of course since I was over already, I thought I might as well pop over to Paris and have a look for the silly dress. She's been on and on about the dress since she saw it on Anne Pallas this spring at her sister's birthday party. It's mighty pricey I can tell you."

Chloe was well aware of how Hyacinth doted on her two daughters, Juliette and Olivia. They were both within a few years of Chloe's age, and well used to whatever society had to offer. Chloe had heard many stories of the younger Wiggenham's during the ship's voyage. She stifled a giggle at the thought of the ever-untidy Hyacinth popping anywhere, and inquired about the much sought after garment.

"Yes, I did finally get my hands on the thing," Hyacinth admitted in response to Chloe's question. "But let me tell you, it's gotta be shipped back home, and our own dress maker is going to have to do a job of fitting her. Juliette is a mighty small girl and has always had trouble with the fittings. She would have come herself, but with all them parties and dances now that she's almost 18 it was better that she didn't. Of course Olivia would have gone in a flash, but at her age she needs to be figuring out what she wants to do with herself."

"Well, I am just so glad you are here Hyacinth. I admit that it's been an amazing trip so far, but it's nice to see a friend besides Mrs. Mainthswaite." Indeed Chloe had been mourning the loss of the camaraderie on the ship. Once in London, that was gone, and with the additional loss of Mr. Haydon's genial company, the evenings had been quite quiet in Paris.

The two ladies chatted on until Mrs. Mainthswaite joined them for dinner. Chloe found herself telling Hyacinth of all the sights they had seen and the impressions they had made on her. She filled her in on their activities and made an amusing tale out of the visit to Mrs. Mainthswaite's cousins. Mrs. Mainthswaite, who had been unaware of Chloe's nocturnal wanderings with Maggie had chuckled as Chloe related the story. The ladies discovered that they were all travelling back to London within a day of each other and that although Chloe would be leaving soon after, they could spend a few days in each other's company in London.

Dinner passed pleasantly and even Mrs. Mainthswaite shared some amusing anecdotes and joined in with stifled smiles at the alarming headgear on a fellow diner. Soon it was time for the opera, and although Mrs. Mainthswaite graciously extended an invitation, Hyacinth pleaded tiredness and said that she would most certainly see them in a few days in London. Off into the crisp cold night they went. The stars were sharp in the twilight, and laughter and lights sparkling off of the lamp posts, shimmered brightly. Chloe was unprepared for the grandeur of the opera house. She didn't know where to look first. At the glittering chandeliers hanging high above their heads, the carvings and ornate décor, or the ladies in their Parisian fashions with furs and feathers, jewels twinkling in their hair and throats. When she whispered to Mrs. Mainthswaite, she received a smile and a genteel shrug

"Well it is Paris after all." Mrs. Mainthswaite whispered back out of the corner of her mouth.

She had found the theater to be an incredible experience in London, but this went beyond. The decadence of the society ladies outshone the theater. Although she could not understand the words, the gestures and music swept Chloe away. Chloe paid polite attention to Mrs. Mainthswaite's group of friends during the intermission, but Chloe could not keep her eyes from taking in as much as she could. The night flew in a blur of crystal, lights and feathers, and before she knew it, it had come time to say goodbye to the opera house. The cold air greeted them like an old friend and accompanied them back to their hotel amid darkened streets.

Chapter 21

Gray light filtered into the room creeping under Chloe's eyelids. For a moment she wasn't sure where she was, but then remembered she was back in London in her wonderfully warm and soft bed. Lying among the blankets and feeling quite cozy, Chloe let her thoughts wander. Tomorrow she could seek out Hyacinth, who had several days until she returned to her own grand house across the ocean. Chloe almost wished she were returning as well. Almost. She chided herself for her feeling, knowing full well that this may be the only time she would cross the sea, and most certainly in such a comfortable manner. However much she reminded herself of her luck, there was a growing part of her that heartily wished to be back in her small third floor room among such dear friends as Fiona and James. Although she had become closer to Mrs. Mainthswaite in the past weeks and regarded the older lady with a fondness which surprised her, she was lonely for companions of her own age. In only two weeks they would begin the long journey back to New York, and Chloe knew her excitement would keep her buoyed as the hours would be long. She closed her eyes and pictured James, his bright blue eyes searching deep into hers and his warm slow smile he reserved only for her. Wrenching her thoughts back to her present, Chloe rose and dressed quickly in the chilly morning. Pulling the curtains aside, she saw that it was still quite early; the traffic on the broad cross street was light. After a solitary breakfast in her room with her journal, Chloe tapped on Mrs. Mainthswaite's door, entering when bidden.

The work for the morning was light. Chloe had finished what she intended by ten o'clock, and spend some time watching the street scenes from Mrs. Mainthswaite's broad window, while her employer was buried in a sheaf of papers. The tiny clock chimed the half hour and Mrs. Mainthswaite emerged from her labors to announce that she had a luncheon meeting with Mr. Haydon. Chloe was overjoyed to hear the news.

"I'm so glad Mrs. Mainthswaite. He must have missed you while we were in Paris." Mrs. Mainthswaite gave a delicate snort and once again delved into her reading. Chloe couldn't help but smile and felt a twinge of excitement. She certainly hoped the luncheon boded well for both parties involved. Chloe gathered her things and prepared to leave the room when Mrs. Mainthswaite rather unnecessarily started to explain the reason for the lunch. "It is a business lunch, nothing more. I have decided to sell two of Edward's business ventures and Mr. Haydon, in attempting to extend his interests to America, has given me an offer which I have been considering." Mrs. Mainthswaite looked suspiciously flushed as she said this, but since she offered no more of an explanation, Chloe left the room with a knowing smile at her employer, who avoided Chloe's eyes. Once alone in hers, she collapsed on her bed stifling a giggle. Chloe tried to imagine what kind of offer Mr. Haydon had given her, but she was unable to picture Mrs. Mainthswaite with any more than her usual sardonic smile, so she gave up.

Chloe decided to bundle up, brave the chill and go for a walk in the wonderful park she had discovered early in their stay in London. The park had several lovely ponds and the trees were shading to gold and red. From time to time the leaves floated down in the breeze, creating little islands of floating color on the ponds. Several ducks happily splashed in the nearest pond. Chloe spent several pleasant hours in the park, striking up a conversation with a flaxen haired nanny whose young charges screamed with delight as they pounced on piles of leaves that had blown to and fro in the night. The children invited Chloe to play catch with a ball they brought, which Chloe gladly accepted. She found that the nanny, Letty, not much younger than herself was an intelligent conversationalist and quite ambitious. She was not only the nanny for these rambunctious children, but also tutored the eldest son, and eagerly shared with Chloe her plans for her future. Chloe in turn shared her own plans with Letty and explained how she came to be in London. The afternoon flew by. Chloe was glad to have shared it with someone so alike. The next day Hyacinth would be back, and Chloe looked forward to several cozy afternoons spent with her friend before Hyacinth left for America.

That evening found Mrs. Mainthswaite closeted in her room. When Chloe tapped on the adjoining door to inquire about dinner, she received a vague excuse of a headache. Not easily believing this, Chloe didn't pursue it further, knowing the older lady was even more private than she was. She ate a solitary but not lonely dinner and then spent a quiet evening, writing about the day's activities, in good company with the hazy moon shining though her window.

The next day, after her morning duties, which she completed alone, Chloe hastened over a few blocks in the rain to Hyacinth's hotel see if her friend had arrived back in the city. The kindly concierge in the lobby had given Chloe concise directions to the hotel after she had showed him the piece of paper Hyacinth had provided. On the way, Chloe pondered the reason for Mrs. Mainthswaite's uncharacteristically unexplained absence and hoped that she would know the reason for it very soon. Chloe valued the camaraderie that had sprung up between the two women over the course of the last few weeks, and hoped it was not lost.

Chloe joyfully found her friend had arrived last night and the two spend a wonderful afternoon closeted in the small lounge that was half hidden off of the main hall in Hyacinth's hotel. The fire crackled cheerfully as rain lashed against the windows as the two sipped hot tea and spoke of nothing but trivial matters.

The next few days stayed dismally rainy. Chloe had noticed that it did seem to rain more in London than New York, but generally it was not too bad. The cold rain dampened spirits and even Chloe could not feel as enthusiastic as before. The weather had so concerned Mrs. Mainthswaite that she had decided to book passage a week earlier than expected. "I do hope you are not too disappointed, Chloe but I feel more comfortable if we are back in New York before the end of the month. I don't believe the weather will turn much worse, but the ocean can be quite rough."

"Of course, I am not disappointed, Mrs. Mainthswaite. You have given me an experience of a lifetime. You are the best person to judge the timing, and as long as you feel quite comfortable and have had sufficient time for your business to be concluded, then that is the most important thing."

Chloe half hoped that now she would finally hear what was on Mrs. Mainthswaite's mind, and she was not disappointed in that. As Chloe finished preparing a letter for her employer, she looked up to see Mrs. Mainthswaite with an almost girlish blush. The last few days had passed with almost no contact with Mrs. Mainthswaite, but now it seemed that at last she was satisfied with whatever inner battle she had been fighting.

"Chloe I have come to a decision which has kept me up most nights the last two weeks. It is a decision which will benefit both my late husband's businesses, which are in need of attention; and myself as well. She rose and paced the room a few times, coughed once or twice and continued. "In a few months' time, Mr. Haydon desires to make his permanent residence in America, especially since he has decided to take up the reins of Edward's two businesses. Since I am still involved in both ventures this should prove quite simple. He hopes that with his publishing company behind us, we can increase the business in both England and America. In the process of making these decisions, William has asked me to marry him. After long deliberation, I have accepted.

Chloe let her breath out in a whoosh, unaware of having been holding it. She exclaimed in delight and rushed to the other side of the room to embrace Mrs. Mainthswaite. She almost checked herself at the last moment from being overly affectionate, but she saw that Mrs. Mainthswaite returned the embrace and seemed touched by the spontaneous gesture.

"We have not worked out the details quite yet, but of course I will let you know in due course. With his influence and expertise in publishing, this may very well be an excellent opportunity for you, my dear." Her eyes twinkled. "I am sure you have been very diligent in your journal writing and I look forward to reading some more stories like that of Philippe and his guitar. You may well ask what I am thinking of marrying at my age." Mrs. Mainthswaite gave a delicate cough. "I have been wondering the same thing."

"Oh no Mrs. Mainthswaite I think it's wonderful! I hardly know what to say. I am just glowing with happiness for both you and Mr. Haydon. What an exciting trip this has been! Even more so I mean!" Chloe became quite rambling in her happiness, but Mrs. Mainthswaite waved her off and told her to run along and visit her friend. Chloe fairly ran the three blocks to Hyacinth's hotel, dodging rain drops and surprised pedestrians.

"Well look at you, half drowned and windblown. What's the rush?" Hyacinth looked up, hidden behind a large afghan of unspeakably ugly green and gold wool that she was knitting. The rain drops which had accumulated on Chloe's skirt and hat steamed unpleasantly as she stood, breathless, with her hands stretched toward the crackling fire in Hyacinth's lushly appointed room.

"You will never guess!" Chloe plumped herself in the chair nearest the fire as soon as her hands had warmed enough to bring pins and needles. "Mrs. Mainthswaite is getting married! Isn't that wonderful?"

Hyacinth settled more comfortably in her chair, dislodging the woolen mound on her lap. "Well this is news. Who is the new suitor? She certainly never mentioned anything to me in Paris." Although Mrs. Mainthswaite would probably have rather endured several uncomfortable voyages across the Channel than to disclose her personal information to Hyacinth, the latter seemed quite surprised she was not informed sooner. "Is she planning on staying in London then?" Hyacinth asked after hearing an abridged version of the romance from Chloe.

"No, no." Chloe shook her head. "She is decidedly coming back; in fact she has changed the date of our departure because she was afraid the seas may turn rough. There is a boat leaving in five days." She leaned back enjoying the soft chair and the heat of the fire on her feet. Hyacinth pushed a plate of cakes toward her.

"Well that's just sweet ain't it? Although to be married at that age." Hyacinth frowned. "Well to each his own. I could see her married to an Englishman to be sure. She's always so prim and proper. Now, what about you?"

"What about me?" Chloe stammered, unable to stop the rising red stain on her cheeks.

"Oh come, Chloe, every time you speak about your James your eyes gets all dreamy. You may play dumb my girl, but I know you have some kinda understanding with him. You may not like to talk too much about yourself but that doesn't mean I can't see it clear as day. I raised two daughters didn't I?"

Chloe affirmed that she had indeed raised two daughters. She looked down for a moment. True she and James had an understanding, so she hoped. It had been after all quite a few weeks since that wonderful kiss. "Yes we have an understanding. I think. At least I think we did when I left. It's been …complicated."

"Good gracious girl, it's always complicated. Why when me and Johnnie were going together, he did everything in the world not to let me get involved in his life. Said it wasn't suitable for a young thing like me. Well I put a stop to all his nonsense. After that, it took a lot to keep us apart"

Chloe couldn't help chucking as she imagined a young Hyacinth getting her way.

"He feels the same way as you do I imagine? Or does he too feel it's too complicated." Hyacinth poked fun at her young friend but her motherly gaze softened her words.

"Well, I think he does. But, oh I don't know, I was so silly before. When I went back home when my sister was sick, I pushed him away. I didn't know what I wanted. I only wanted to be independent. Now, I just hope he still feels the way he did when I left. I came out to the city to find my life, and to find where I fit in, like I have said before, and he wasn't planned for. This…" At a loss for works Chloe subsided into silence and stared at the fire.

Hyacinth nodded understandingly. "I know dearie, you just got on your own two feet and now he comes along making you feel so …helpless like. Unsettled, that's the word. But you don't have to give up your freedom Chloe. James loves you for who you are." Hyacinth grinned at Chloe's slow blush. "Yes, I think he does and so do you. The point is, if he wanted some helpless little chit who giggled brainlessly, well there are a hundred times as many of them. But he doesn't. He wants you. So quit your dithering about and just see what happens when you return to New York. That's all you can do. Why, when I was a young girl, I was the same way, only not so educated as you. I worked in a shop and made a wage, not only because of my folks, but because I wanted to be independent, not that that was very acceptable in my day. Well, when I met Johnnie I told him right off the bat that I wasn't waiting on him like some housemaid. He always did have some common sense and he agreed. Before he made his money we had some tight times." Hyacinth had been from a working class family, and had faced hardships such as Chloe had not known, before marrying an enterprising young man who turned a coach rental service into a fortune.

Greatly heartened by Hyacinth's wise and honest words, Chloe felt hear heart lighten considerably. The two ladies passed onto lighter subjects, and subsequently spend the rest of that afternoon and the next in cozy conversation. Hyacinth rehashed many exciting adventures from her younger days, and Chloe caught a glimpse of the adventurous young woman her friend must have been. The time passed all too quickly, for the next day Hyacinth would be embarking on her return voyage. Chloe prepared to take her leave, both ladies promising to keep in touch with letters and visits.

Chapter 22

The last days in England passed in a blur. The rain stopped for a longer length of time and wan sunshine filtered through the clouds, bringing milder temperatures than they had since coming back from Paris. Chloe was glad to be leaving at the end of the week. The trip had been magical and exceeded Chloe's very detailed dreams of voyaging over the sea; but she was ready to go home. She would always treasure the sights and sounds which had now become so dear to her. Her memories would have a special place, always in that time just before falling asleep as she reviewed her day.

Mrs. Mainthswaite was very busy for the remainder of the stay. Mr. Haydon occupied much of her time of course as they remained closeted in his offices for large amounts of the day. There was much to discuss between the two, as well as many business details to smooth out. He remained as charming as ever to Chloe, insisting she call him by his first name, William, a request she felt was difficult to obey. Chloe was not left alone at all during this last week, however busy Mrs. Mainthswaite was. Mr. Haydon had gone to great lengths to make sure she was escorted to many afternoon gatherings, including three afternoon teas with friends of his. Chloe enjoyed all of the activities and being one who was a great observer of human nature stored every experience away in her head to be examined and mulled over later in the evening in the company of her journal. She was also surprised and gratified to find that Mrs. Mainthswaite had shown her little story about the French gentleman to

Mr. Haydon who promptly declared it to be "charmingly unique" and asked Chloe if she would like to see it in next month's publication. This was a feather in Chloe's literary cap, and she could not express enough gratitude to Mr. Haydon.

As Chloe sat at her window on the last day in England, she thought back to the very beginning of the journey, and wondered at the immeasurable knowledge and experience she had gained. She felt like an intrepid explorer coming home triumphantly to report on her wondrous weeks abroad. Nevertheless, once her mind was quiet in the dim light of the moon, she felt just as young and scared and excited as ever when she thought about what she was coming home to. James was there, and no one could tell Chloe exactly if they would continue where they left off, or what was to come after. She thought about that for a while, and of James, who did not expect her to leave England yet for another week. After imagining so many different outcomes to her homecoming, she sighed in exasperation, dreading the next morning if she could not get to sleep, and punched her pillow again into a more comfortable shape. Eventually she drifted into a fitful sleep, but even there James flitted from dream to dream.

The next morning Chloe felt as gray as the thick fog that blanketed the city and made it difficult to see the end of the street. When they finally settled on board the majestic ship, she felt exhausted by the morning of waiting and standing and retired to her cabin to stare at nothing and doze. Mrs. Mainthswaite could hardly help but notice Chloe's lethargy, but wisely made no comment. However much their relationship had grown, Chloe still would have hesitated to lay her own romantic inclinations on her employer.

Chapter 23

    The ballroom was as grand, glittering and elegant as on Chloe's first voyage. The soft string music filled the air and lulled Chloe into a peaceful contentment. She chatted with her table mates and laughed along with their jests. Thankfully there were no indolent young men to ward off. Chloe was left to her own devices a good part since there was not much to do for Mrs. Mainthswaite in a professional capacity. All of their preparations had gone off splendidly for the visit to England. Once back, there was still work to be done of course, but naturally Chloe wondered a bit what effect Mrs. Mainthswaite's marriage would have on her employment. Although she had not said as much to her employer, Mrs. Mainthswaite brought the subject up on her own during luncheon on the second day aboard the ship. She assured Chloe that in fact her work would probably increase with the combination of Mr. Haydon's knowledge and company and Mrs. Mainthswaite's references. Chloe's future looked bright indeed. This was what Chloe had longed for and worked toward when she moved to New York. Despite these assurances, Chloe thought with trepidation of their return and what future lay ahead for her and James. It was an exciting yet terrifying thought.

Once they had gotten used to the sway of the ship, Chloe and Mrs. Mainthswaite staked out a comfortable corner in the saloon most days as it was too cold to sit outside on deck. It was a cheerful and warm compartment, bookshelves lined the wall near their corner and the red leather furniture was soft enough to sink in and doze off over a book. It was not a very crowded area, yet Chloe found that she was able to indulge in one of her favorite pastimes, people watching, as much as she wanted. She found that after spending the better part of two months in their company, those in the upper echelons of society were not nearly as interesting as those in the working class. For the most part, most of the ladies seemed to be of the same mold. They dressed alike, each competing with her neighbor for the most fashionable dress which resulted in exceedingly similar costumes. They all giggled and laughed, fluttering their eyelashes in a rather shallow fashion. Chloe was sure that behind closed doors, each society maid was interesting in her own way but wished they were able to show more individuality in public. Chloe preferred to strike up conversations with some of the third class passengers. She found some interesting companions in this way, and wrote several small stories about their situations. She showed these to Mrs. Mainthswaite who promptly confiscated them telling Chloe that she wanted to have Mr. Haydon put them in his magazine, much to Chloe's delight. There was no one quite as interesting as Hyacinth on this trip however, and Chloe felt glad about that. The world could probably only handle one Hyacinth Wiggenham at a time.

The last banquet of course was the opportunity for everyone to wear their finest. Chloe wore her best pink gown, paired with a heavy ivory silk shawl of Mrs. Mainthswaite's and her pearl necklace, which now was a world traveler like her. The guests all had the faintly saddened air, as they said their goodbye's to acquaintances. Chloe exchanged her address with a few other girls her age, but did not feel that any long lasting friendship would come of it. The evening passed pleasantly and once again Chloe was closeted in her cubbyhole cabin. The moon was dim in her tiny porthole, and made no night light for Chloe, but the rocking of the ship soon lulled her to sleep despite her trepidation about the following day.

Chapter 24

By the time they had made their way through the throngs of people noisily jostling one another in their eagerness to reach family members, Chloe felt as if she had been battered on all sides. The crowds had not been so intense when they had docked in England. She clung to her carryall firmly as she pushed her way through the crowd, keeping Mrs. Mainthswaite's elegantly attired silver head in view. Numb with anticipation, finally she reached where Mrs. Mainthswaite was waiting for the carriage. Once it trundled into view, they climbed aboard and Chloe sat looking out at the familiar streets with a new appreciation and sense of homecoming so strong it made a lump in her throat. Mrs. Mainthswaite rested her head against the seat and seemed glad to be home. The knowledge of what was shortly to come had kept her buoyed throughout the voyage and Chloe knew that however tightly her employer held her feelings to herself she must be jubilated but saddened to find herself half a world away from Mr. Haydon, at least for the next few months.

They neared Mrs. Mainthswaite's dignified home and Chloe's heart continued to climb until it was in danger of jumping right out of her throat. Once Mrs. Mainthswaite had gone into her house, Chloe would be left alone with her thoughts, almost at the end of a journey of a lifetime.

"You may have the day off tomorrow Chloe. I expect you will have some unpacking and catching up to do. When gone this long, we all need to settle back into every day routines." Mrs. Mainthswaite spoke suddenly in the silence, rousing herself from her own private thoughts. Chloe flashed her a grateful smile, unable to speak for fear she may not be able to control the emotions which ran through her. The carriage stopped on the quiet street which was so familiar, now lined with almost bare russet colored trees. Chloe helped her employer down from the high step and stood idly while the driver unloaded her trunks and bags, carrying them through the front door with a tip of his cap. Grace had emerged at the sound of the wheels and rushed forward to hug Chloe warmly. Chloe returned this with enthusiasm, longing to stop and chatter with Grace and find out about the household in their absence. She had missed Grace and Mrs. Kingston immensely. Too soon, however, the driver was ready and as he looked enquiringly at her she waved goodbye to Grace and Mrs. Mainthswaite and climbed back in the carriage. They rushed toward her part of the city with what seemed like unprecedented speed and too soon they had pulled up before her boardinghouse as if she had never left at all. The streets were as busy as ever, now people wearing coats and warmer clothes of course. She saw no one familiar as she climbed down and waited for her trunk and carryall. Breathing deeply, she reminded herself that this was a Tuesday and her friends were all working at this time of the day. No one knew she was even back. It was another day, like every other in the city; except for her it felt so different. Numbly she brought her carryall up the narrow stairs and into her room, preceded by the driver with her trunk. She could feel the quietness of the house close around her. She spent some time looking around her room, surprised that it looked perhaps. The coverlet on her bed still had the slight wrinkles in it from the last morning, when she had sat upon the foot of it while finishing her last minute packing. The air was chilly, and there was the forlorn look a room acquires when it hasn't been used. Finally hefting her trunk onto the table she unpacked the top layer, bringing out some small knick knacks and setting them in a row along the window sill. She purchased small items for James, Fiona, and Mrs. Hall and also brought a tiny picture postcard for Grace and Mrs. Kingston, as well as her brothers. She also had bought a silk scarf for her sister, and had decided at the last moment to purchase an ink well for her father, with an engraving on it. She had gotten one for herself and knew that however much he may grumble, secretly he would be touched. She felt that she probably spent more than she should have on her souvenirs but it was quite a special occasion. She looked at all of the knick knacks and decided to abandon the rest of her unpacking for the moment. It could wait. Her mind was whirling with memories of her adventure, and also with thoughts of what was to come. She told herself sternly to stop acting like a ninny. She knew it was all because she felt so hesitant and so eager to see James, and nothing she could do would help her feeling that way, except to go see him and hope that they shared the same thoughts. She decided to go down the hall and pay a visit to her landlady, and then stop by to see Fiona, as well as pick up a few supplies for the week. Mrs. Hall was surprised to see her back a week early, and anxious about the dust in the room.

"I was planning on having it clean as a whistle for you when you came back. Oh dear I hope it's not too dusty."

Mrs. Hall lamented. Chloe assured her that it was perfectly fine, turned down an offer for a cup of tea and made her way out into the street. As she walked through the bustle of people, she smiled to herself. It was good to be back. She could hardly wait to see Fiona, and quickened her pace.

Fiona was indeed in the shop today, patiently waiting for an elderly woman in a scruffy wool coat to decide which kind of sugar to purchase. When at last the lady settled on her choice, along with a few other necessities, and left the store, trundling past Chloe with her heavy basket, Chloe stepped forward amid squeals of delight from Fiona. Ignoring the disapproving stares from other customers and the warning 'ahem' from her father, Fiona rushed forward enveloping her friend in a fierce hug.

"Chloe, what are you doing here? I thought your shop would dock NEXT week! Has anything happened?"

Chloe laughingly put up a hand to ward off further questions, and replied "Mrs. Mainthswaite decided to come earlier and take advantage of the warm fall in London. She was hesitant to travel any later for fear of bad weather or ice." Chloe beamed at the warm reception from her friend despite her shaky emotions. She felt as if she would burst from gladness at seeing Fiona's dear face. "Plus she had quite an eventful trip, but I'll fill you in on that later." Chloe added glancing at the motions Fiona's father was making toward the counter. "I am so happy to see you Fiona. You look well." She hugged Fiona again and noted indeed Fiona's smile and sparkling eyes matched the tiny gleam on her ring finger, which had a lot to do with Fiona's happiness. "How is

James?" Chloe couldn't help but ask although she knew she ought to let Fiona back to work.

"Um, He...He's good. Working hard though. Look I have to go. Come over tonight! Please!" We'll have time to talk then." Fiona backed toward the counter as her father let out a sigh of exasperation, although he grinned at Chloe good humoredly, since he knew how close the girls were. "We'll talk tonight! I know James missed you." Fiona gave her a knowing little smile before running back.

Chloe nodded and waved at Fiona's father on her way out, feeling no less nervous but heartened at Fiona's words. James missed her, how did Fiona know? Did James tell her so? Did he give Fiona an indication of his feelings? Chloe wished that tonight was here already and started back home determined to finish her unpacking and keep her mind busy. She decided to accept that cup of tea from Mrs. Hall.

Chloe went back out of the store into the busy street. The bright sunlight made the shadows sharp and brought out the dusty smudges on the store windows. She felt better than she had in several days, having seen Fiona had done her good. Plus Fiona had said James missed her. That felt good. Was he working? Chloe wondered what he was doing at the moment. Should she try walking over to his room? It was not too many blocks away? But no, this evening she would catch up with Fiona first.

"I'll see you tonight! I'm so glad you're home!" Fiona had popped her head out of the door and her high clear voice carried to Chloe like a bell. Chloe waved her hand in acknowledgement and carried on, expertly sidestepping a runaway peddler's cart. Back at her room, she found Mrs. Hall with dust cloth in hand attacking Chloe's room with gusto. Chloe offered to help, and together they dusted and swept the room, even cleaning the window so that the sun shone through, leaving a bright square on the broad wood planks of the floor.

"It looks much better Mrs. Hall. Thank you. And now how about that cup of tea? For the dust." Chloe twinkled as her landlady laughed at the mild joke.

"Ah the dust indeed, we'll be needing that tea now I might say. Shall we just go into the front room then?" Mrs. Hall led the way to her own apartment and Chloe followed bringing the small trinket she had purchased for Mrs. Hall in London. The two ladies spent a cozy hour, catching up on the latest gossip. After tea, with a fresh cake Mrs. Hall had just baked the day before, Chloe determined to finish unpacking and run out to the shop nearby since she had forgotten completely to buy food while at Fiona's store. Finishing these proved to be exhausting, and it was not until evening when Chloe finally sat down, after getting in a few staples for her tiny pantry. As she walked back from the store, the smell drifting out of the bakery up the street had been so enticing that she had to go in, and despite her heavy basket, and buy the bread. That night she would have some of the hearty bread and cheese. She had gotten unused to such simple dinners in her travels, but it felt good to be home. All of the activity had kept Chloe's mind from wandering too much although thoughts of James did pop up unwarranted from time to time. She let them come, knowing that it was no use to try and push them away. Bringing her plate to her table, she wrote a letter to her sister as she munched on the crusty flavorful bread. She would have to send a parcel with the gifts, once she was settled at Mrs. Mainthswaite's again. She quickly changed her skirt, as she was still in her travel clothes, and walked quickly over to Fiona's, shivering in the sharp autumn evening.

"Oh, come in Chloe." Fiona's mother smiled warmly as she gave Chloe a quick hug. "Fiona is so pleased you are home. Please go into the kitchen, she is just drying the dishes. How was your trip?" Her mother followed Chloe in, listening as she gave a brief description of the ship, and their time in London and Paris. "My, it all sounds so wonderful and adventurous. But now you are back and ready to settle down." Fiona's mother was happy to have Fiona engaged, and assumed that was the aspiration of all young ladies. "Yes Mrs. Walsh." Chloe smiled and picked up a spare dish cloth, ready to help.

The girls finished the dishes and stacked them away on the high shelf over the worn table. Then Fiona led Chloe into the small room which she shared with her younger sister, under the eaves. They had the room to themselves fortunately, since Fiona's sister was visiting with the elderly lady who rented their extra bedroom.

"I want to hear absolutely everything about your trip Chloe, but I have the feeling that if we don't talk about James you are going to burst. Is that right?" Chloe nodded, her eyes shining.

"Yes. You see, when James came to see me off, right before I went away, James was, well, he…he kissed me." Chloe took a look at Fiona's astonished and delighted face. "It was very fast, and soft, and wonderful."

"Did you kiss him back?"

Chloe nodded and told her how it happened. "I have been thinking of that moment for the entire trip, you see."

"Of course I see." Fiona then arranged her features into a look which showed her vast experience as an engaged woman. "Now you see how he feels about you."

"Well I did. I mean, it's been quite a while, and I had hoped to see him…" Chloe trailed off, not knowing quite what else she could say about the situation.

"Chloe," Fiona's face shadowed over. "James has gotten a new job. He wrote to me not quite three weeks ago."

"Oh? Where is this? I know he had been hoping for something." Chloe was happy to hear this but troubled by Fiona's somber face.

"It's not…really in the city. It's temporary though." Fiona quickly added, seeing the look of alarm spread over her friend's face and turning the smile into a tight thin line.

"How temporary? And where?"

"I don't know exactly where, but I know it's not more than a few hours from the city on the train. He doesn't think you will be back for another week, I am sure he had planned to come back next weekend when you were to arrive. "

Chloe felt like a bolt of lightning had hit her chest and she could hardly draw a breath.

"It's a town north of the city, but I don't know what it's called. Not big at all from what he said in his letter. It's not permanent. Chloe don't look so distraught. He will be back. Soon. I am sure he may come home Friday."

Chloe shook her head. "What if he isn't back? No, I can't wait. I must go there. I can go tomorrow and be back. Mrs. Mainthswaite is not expecting me."

"No Chloe you can't just go. I told you, I don't even know the name of the town, much less what he is doing. You can't just show up in a strange town."

"Yes I can. That's how I arrived here."

"But you at least knew what New York was called." Said Fiona practically. "How do we know if the train is regular? Likely it's not. If it's a small town such as he indicated. How do we know where?"

"I can find out. Perhaps Mrs. Mainthswaite would be agreeable to my borrowing her carriage but that may take some time."

"Chloe, it's just not possible. You must be patient"

Chloe smiled affectionately at her concerned friend. "Fiona, I've wasted enough time figuring out my own mind though. I don't want to wait any more."

"That's all well and good, but for the fact that we do not know where he is and like I keep saying it's very temporary."

Chloe hung her head. The truth of Fiona's words finally making an impression on her "That's true unfortunately." She said mournfully

Chloe was silent for a moment, thinking. She could feel herself succumbing to Fiona's practical advice even though every fiber of her body wanted to go find James. "Where would he stay when he comes here this weekend? If he comes."

Fiona rolled her eyes affectionately at her friend. "He'll come. He will stay in his room of course. He kept it, you can't let such a room go, he might not find another one at such a rent. I told you, this is a temporary job. He must need to earn more money than he is earning from his writing."

Chloe considered this and felt better to hear that he had kept his room in the city. She had been so dismayed at finding him gone, she had not thought about the practicalities. "Very well Fiona. I will wait until this Friday."

Fiona smiled and gave Chloe a swift and comforting hug "I'm glad you agree Chloe. And it will be fine. I promise. From what you have told me about you and James on the day you departed, I should think his feelings are fairly clear. And no more worries about if he has changed them! I don't want to hear it!"

Chloe giggled, relieved and touched by her friend's faith. "Thank you Fiona. You are a dear, dear friend."

Filling Fiona in on the details of her trip took Chloe's mind off of James for an hour or two. Ducking to avoid the pillow Fiona had thrown, Chloe stood and stretched, her fingers grazing the sloping low ceiling. "I would love to stay longer, but it's getting late. Oh! But I completely forgot. I have something for you. I left it at home in my haste. "

"That's all right Chloe; Hank is coming by tomorrow evening. He does at least three times a week." At this statement Chloe rolled her eyes at Fiona, poking fun at her complacent air. "We will stop by tomorrow evening. I have to make up for lost time with my best friend." She waved her hand at Chloe who ducked out of the door and followed her down the narrow staircase, stopping to bid Fiona's parents good night.

The next day crawled by with an agonizing anticipation that would not abate. Chloe straightened her room for the tenth time and wished that Mrs. Mainthswaite had not given her the day off. Although the day was cold, with steely clouds and a persistent wind. Chloe went for a walk in the old park, where everything had started. It looked forlorn. There were dead buds on the bushes, and although it looked as though someone had taken time to sweep the sidewalk, the brown leaves stuck against the iron fence gave it unkempt look. That evening Fiona did drop in with Hank in tow. He was just as quiet as ever, but with a ready smile and chuckle. The trio had a cup of coffee to warm them and listened to the creaking house, as the wind tried to find a way in. Being a fairly well built house, it was not unduly cold. Chloe spent some time informing Fiona of Mrs. Mainthswaite's surprising news, which she had neglected to mention the night before. Fiona gasped in all the right places, and clasped Chloe to her with pride at hearing of Chloe's very promising future with William Haydon's backing and connections.

"It's exactly what I have been working for, Fiona." Chloe felt her heart warm at the thought of the future, even with her uncertainties for the coming weekend.

During the next two days, Chloe went to Mrs. Mainthswaite's. She enjoyed a cheery reunion with Mrs. Kingston and Grace, and spent a few happy hours in the warm kitchen, smelling the enticing pastry and delicious stews long before they were ready. Chloe felt, however happy she was to be home, that agonizing slowness of the clock, and was determined that Friday afternoon would never come. Finally it did however. She took her leave quickly. Not wanting to prolong it, although she could tell that Grace was eager to discuss what may or may not happen. She hurried home and ate a quick meal. Not because she was hungry, but because she knew she must. It had been hours since lunch. Her nerves were electric with anticipation. She left her house at about a quarter to six , having bundled up, with a woolen shawl over her new rust colored suit, stuffing her threadbare gloves in the pocket of her coat.

She remembered where James lived, and since it was not more than 25 minutes, she walked. The air was chilly but not unduly so for autumn. The wind, playfully blowing the dusty sidewalks clean, would hopefully clear some of the cobwebs from her mind which was occupied solely with the daunting task ahead of her. She managed to convince herself that he would arrive, although it may be quite late. As she walked, she took deep breaths to calm herself. Lost in her thoughts, she realized in no time at all that she had turned the corner of his street, and saw his boarding house attached to a row of other nondescript houses. She knew his window was the second from the left, but it was dark. She expected it to be, but still a pang of disappointment shot through her. She climbed the three stairs to the front stoop of his boarding house, moved aside a neglected umbrella and sat, after brushing off the step. It appeared that his landlady was not as zealous about sweeping the stoop as Mrs. Hall. She settled herself as comfortably as she could on the cold surface and tucked her heavy skirt around her legs. As it wasn't that chilly, she put her shawl aside for later. Few people passed by. It was a quieter street than hers. Some people glanced at her curiously but walked by intent on their own business. The street darkened noticeably as the twilight deepened and the lamps above her went on, one by one. Chloe waited still, pulled her shawl around her shoulders and leaned against the porch rail. It was quiet, and she watched lights in houses turn on, then off. She wondered if she should leave, but decided to stay for a bit more. It was a comfortable nook that she had wedged herself into and not too cold either. She sat, alone with her thoughts, for quite some time, and then not even realizing, her head drooped, and her eyes closed. Had anyone walked by at that time of night, the small figure in the deep shadow of the porch would not have been noticed.

Light forced its way between closed eyelids. Chloe moved, and then felt the stiffness of her neck and legs. She opened her eyes, not comprehending that she had, in fact, fallen asleep, on the doorstep of James' boardinghouse. Looking around she surmised that it was still quite early, and then disappointment hit her. James had not come back, for it was hardly likely that he would have practically trodden over her to reach his room. She stood, massaging her aching neck and shoulders, and stretched. Taking one last look at the closed door, with its peeling paint, she turned to begin her walk home, sadness weighing her down. A lone figure had turned the corner, and for a moment Chloe almost imagined that it was James. The familiar loping walk came toward her, but then it could have been any young man with hat pulled down in the early morning dawn. She studied him for a second, watching as he came closer. The realization dawned on her that it was James. He had not caught sight of her since she was still hidden in the shadow of the overhanging roof. Her heart thumped wildly, and she could barely catch her breath as she watching his dear figure come closer. She stepped forward to see if he would see her, but, head still lowered to the ground, intent upon his walk, he did not. Not until he was coming up the short walk to the porch did he realize that there was another figure standing. Chloe coughed gently and James looked up. He stared in amazement for several long seconds, while Chloe fidgeted, not knowing what to do. Finally, with what seemed like an explosion of movement, he had covered the last few feet to the porch and crushed her in his arms so tightly that she gasped.

"Chloe?" James finally spoke, his voice hoarse with bewilderment and shock. "You're here! Really here?" Chloe, still enfolded in his arms could feel his heart beating hard. She craned her neck, but could not see his face, could not see that shining eyes that looked down upon her head.

"We took an earlier ship."

At last James relinquished her from the vice-like hug and held her at arm's length, searching her face as if it had been years not mere weeks. He pulled her close again, but this time it was tender, warm. "I have missed you Chloe. More than you know."

Chloe hugged back, never wanting to let go, now that they were finally together. "No, I do know how much James." She wanted so much to tell him all of the things she was thinking and feeling. The words jumbled up in her mouth though and would not come. The most important thing was the one thing she could say. "I love you James." She whispered it shyly but with resolution, her face hidden from his so that he couldn't see the tears of emotion shining in her eyes.

She felt James shift, hoped that had not been too forward of her. He pulled away slightly and peeped down into her face, raising it with a finger under her chin. His wonderful blue eyes were shining brilliantly and Chloe knew that she had not been too forward after all. He studied her for what seemed like an eternity. Gently he pushed a few stray locks out of her eyes and whispered back "I love you too Chloe Walters. I've loved you for a long time, you know."

She nodded. "I think I have known. I think I've loved you for a long time as well. I was just afraid of it." She didn't have to tell him why, she knew he would understand.

He cupped her face in his two hands and smiled down at her. "You never have to be afraid." His lips gently but firmly met hers and were confidant of their response.

An elderly woman in a tartan wrap walked by with a stout bull dog on a leash. The woman coughed disapprovingly but they paid her no attention. For all they knew, a day and a night could have gone by. Chloe didn't care about the cold or the stiffness of her neck. She and James had a lot to catch up on. She remained folded in James arms. Finally he stirred so that they could look at each other. Suddenly, as if roused from a dream, he realized the time of morning and the fact that she had been sitting, quite disheveled on his doorstep. "Chloe, were you sitting there all night?"

Chloe laughed a bit shamefully. "I came to see if you were home last night, and well, I fell asleep. Did you take a train?"

Now it was James' turn to laugh. "No, the train was not until this afternoon. I wanted to bring a story back I have been working on for the Times. I was able to hitch a ride with a farmer coming into the city, took a nap in the back of his delivery truck. Then I walked for the last hour. I never thought to see you here at my doorstep this morning though." He looked her over, brushing the wrinkles out of her skirt and straightening her shawl with a familiarity that felt so safe to Chloe. "Chloe you are cold. You have been out all night. Even on a mild night; you're going to catch a cold."

Chloe looked up at James with a smile. "I don't think I'll ever be cold again James. Come, we have a lot to catch up on."

Epilogue

Chloe straightened the collar on her dress for the hundredth time and stood back, peering out of her window to the sunlit street below, early summer breeze gently tugging at her honey toned curls.

"Chloe come away from the window, help me with this." Fiona sat on the other side of the small bedroom holding a gauzy piece of material in her hands. She gestured to Chloe who came over and took the scrap, looking uncertainly at it.

"I would think it should be pinned just so." Chloe looked critically over Fiona's head at the mirror and tentatively pinned the veil over Fiona's dark locks.

"Yes, that looks about right. What do you think?" Fiona sighed, not really listening to Chloe's affirmation. "After all this time, it's hard to believe today is finally here. Two years IS a long engagement. But it was worth it."

Chloe hid her smile at the matronly and slightly foolish look that Fiona always got when speaking of 'her Hank'. "It's beautiful, Fiona. You're beautiful. I can't imagine Hank will be able to take his eyes off of you. Oh I do hope the boys will arrive soon, it wouldn't do to be rushing at the last minute." Chloe turned back to the window, again searching down on the street below. Her anxiety lessened however for soon the sound of the front door and laughter floated up the stairs.

"Have they ever disappointed us?" Fiona twinkled at her best friend, and paused to reach out and take Chloe's hand, with its small pearl shining from her ring finger. "I hear church bells in the distance, it's time to go."

Made in the USA
Middletown, DE
10 September 2023